THE TRANSFORMATION

Wendy had thirteen minutes for her clothes, hair and makeup. She sprang off her bed and started her race against time.

The digital clock had barely clicked to 12:00 when Wendy was carried off in a rush of wind. She felt rattled and confused. She wasn't ready. How was she ever going to make her transformation work?

And then, she had arrived. Somewhere. It didn't seem like she was at any Ball. In fact, she was all alone in what appeared to be a cave. As her eyes adjusted, she could see that she was in a room made out of stone blocks. Where was she? Where was the Blue Moon Ball?

Wendy moved toward the light. At last, she could hear the low murmuring of voices. With all the concentration she could muster, she pushed away everything that had happened to Wendy Hilton in the last few hours. She wiped her mind clean, like an eraser on a blackboard, and filled it with images of the blazing sun on the desert and the shimmering water of the Nile. She imagined being Cleopatra, the most powerful and beautiful woman in all of Egypt in 40 B.C. She was twenty-nine years old and a queen. Wendy walked the last few feet and stepped out of the opening.

At that moment, the full moon moved out from behind a cloud, its radiance reflecting off of Wendy's blue robes, making it seem like she was in a spotlight. There was a gasp from the crowd....

Macy K —
To the Moon...
To Dreams...

J R Stringfel

THE
MOON
KEY

J. R. STAMPFL

SMOOCH **NEW YORK CITY**

SMOOCH ®

November 2005

Published by

Dorchester Publishing Co., Inc.
200 Madison Avenue
New York, NY 10016

ISBN 0-8439-5619-4

Printed in the United States of America.

Visit us on the web at www.smoochya.com.

For my very own W and P,
in honor of flights into fantasy.
What would life be without them?
For D for all of his love and support.
For my father, who loves to talk about dreams.
And for my mother, who has never
stopped dreaming.

Chapter One

Wendy Hilton stood on the fire escape outside her window. A barely noticeable summer breeze whispered against her face. It was almost midnight. Almost June 21. Time to start her first birthday party. For thirteen years, Wendy had hoped that someone would remember her birthday. But no one ever had. This year, she would do it herself.

She pushed her limp dirty-blond hair away from her face with determination and grabbed her basket. She carefully climbed the fire escape looking for her friend, the moon. Whenever she had a terrible day, she went to the roof and found the moon. The immensity of the moon, the mystique of the moon, the iridescent light of the moon always soothed her.

As she reached the tarred rooftop, she gasped. A gigantic orange moon was just rising in the sky. Her heart started pounding. A full moon for her birthday. That had to be an omen. Quickly, she made a birthday wish. She didn't bother to wish that her parents would come back miraculously and find her. For as long as she could remember, every time she had made a wish that had been it. But no more.

Instead, she wished that there was a place, a magical place that she could go to, her own Neverland where she could be the wonderful Wendy she knew had to be inside of her. If she only knew how to let that Wendy out. If she could only learn to fly. How often had she stood on this roof and felt as if she could just take off?

Wendy sighed. Like she had on every other birthday, she wondered how she might have turned out if she hadn't been left by her parents. She picked up the small wicker basket. It looked like something for a doll. She marveled that she had ever been small enough to fit in it. As she had every day of her life, she wondered what had caused her parents to leave her in it, just a few days old, outside of the Shubert Theater wrapped in a white towel embroidered "Hilton Hotel."

Tenderly, Wendy held the now yellowed terry cloth against her cheek. A piece of paper fluttered out of the folds and almost gusted over the edge of the roof. Wendy lunged for it, aghast that she had almost forgotten it was there.

By the light of the rising moon, she stared at it. Scrawled hastily on a Wendy's Restaurant napkin were the words, *Please take care of her. We'll be back.*

Wendy stared at the bold loops of the writing. She had always thought it looked like a man's writing, her father's writing. But it said *We'll be back.* That implied that they had both of been there, both of her parents. But why had they left her? Why couldn't they take care of her? Were they sick? Poor? In danger?

They had to have loved her. *Please take care of*

her... She hadn't been carelessly abandoned. The Family Services counselor who had given her these things had told her that she had been clean, well fed and bundled carefully in the towel. Family Services didn't know her real name so they had nicknamed her for the Wendy's napkin and the Hilton towel. The name had stuck. Wendy often wondered what her real name was.

And there was one more thing that her parents had left her. Wendy fingered the small silver chain around her neck. On it dangled a silver charm, a sliver of a crescent moon. For Wendy it had always been a sliver of hope. For the millionth time, Wendy pictured her mother impulsively taking it off her neck and placing it around her baby's.

A basket, a towel, a napkin and a necklace—that's all her parents had left with her at the stage door. They had promised to come back. Why hadn't they?

The only sensible conclusion she could reach was that they must have died or they would have....

Because her parents had indicated on the note that they were coming back, Family Services had not been allowed to put Wendy up for adoption for several years. Until it was too late. By the time the authorities had decided that Wendy's parents were never coming back, she was an awkward, overweight child who didn't know how to smile. Couples wanted to adopt smiling babies for whom they cared from the beginning. No one wanted her.

By age ten, she had already been bounced around to seven foster families. So when Ralph and Liz had taken her in to be an older sister for their three boys—Ralphie, Joey and Eddie—Wendy had vowed to stay there. She wished she could see Ralph and Liz more, but they worked a lot. However, she had grown to love the boys. They were her family now.

On her thirteenth birthday, Wendy was transfixed by the glowing moon as she fingered her necklace. She thought about all the years she had wasted waiting for her parents to reappear and change her life. Thirteen years was too long to wait. It was time for her to take charge.

She cleared her throat, aware that her hands were shaking. "I, Wendy Hilton, named for a napkin and towel, understand that it is up to me to make my life whatever it is. I realize now that my parents are not coming back to save me. I have to do it on my own. I believe that I am special. Somehow, I will find my magic and use it."

A chill went up Wendy's spine. She could have sworn that the moon was looking right at her. She bundled up her precious possessions and crept downstairs, looking forward to all the things she had planned for her very first birthday celebration.

Chapter Two

It was not your typical party.

Wendy got off the subway at Times Square. Growing up in New York City, she was completely familiar with the underground system. She had been taking it by herself or with the boys since she was ten. But as she got off the train tonight, she found that her knees were shaking.

It wasn't all the people, the noise, or the confusion. She was nervous about what tonight meant to her. She wondered if she could pull it off.

Well, first things first. She found the alley between West 44th and 45th. She stared at the brass stage door of the Shubert Theater. Thirteen years ago she had been left right there in her basket. And now she was back.

She felt light-headed and sat down on a low wall across from the door. Why was this so important to her? What did she expect to learn? Wendy really wasn't sure. She just knew that she'd been wanting to come here for a long time.

Her breathing was barely back to normal when they started arriving: the cast, the crew, the people who worked there. A couple came up hand in hand. Wendy's heart stopped. Her parents might have been like that. They could have been actors in love. But since Wendy had been wrapped in a hotel towel, maybe they were just tourists.

Wendy wasn't sure how much time had passed when she realized that there had been no traffic through the stage door for a while. It must be close to curtain time. Sure enough, it was just after eight o'clock. It should be safe now. She moved up to the doorway on wobbly legs. The same walk her parents had made.

Had her mother hugged her and cried, devastated to leave her? Had her father gritted his teeth as he set down the basket?

She looked up at the lights and the sky. For a second, she had a premonition that she had seen this all before, exactly this, as a baby. Wendy wished she could know for sure.

Suddenly, it was all too much for her. She felt like she might faint. Remembering that she had eaten very little all day, she moved away slowly.

The Wendy's Restaurant was just a few blocks away. This was the second part of her celebration. She had been saving for months for this night. She had promised herself that she would treat herself to whatever she wanted.

Balancing her tray, she found a table. This could have been the very Wendy's where her parents had sat trying to figure out what to do with their new baby. Impulsively, Wendy took out a pen and grabbed a napkin. Just like they had.

June 21
I came back on my thirteenth birthday. Now I
will take care of myself.
—Wendy Hilton

Wendy stored the napkin carefully away in her purse. She took a couple more bites of her burger and then threw everything away, amazed that, for once, she had no appetite.

She quickly walked back to the Shubert Theater, to the front door this time. Just as she arrived, the double doors popped open from the inside and everyone came pouring out. It was intermission, just as she had figured. In all her planning for this night, she hadn't even paid attention to what was playing at the Shubert. She spotted a program that had been dropped on the sidewalk.

A Midsummer Night's Dream by William Shakespeare. Amazing, thought Wendy. She hadn't read any Shakespeare yet. But she knew that her birthday, June 21, was on a special day, the longest day of the year, the shortest night; a midsummer night.

The lights blinked under the marquis. Intermission was over. It was time. Wendy had been fascinated by the theater for a long time. She had read that a lot of young actors saw their first Broadway shows by sneaking into performances at the intermission.

Wendy felt guilty about sneaking in, but she never could have afforded a ticket. If a seat was empty, what was the harm?

Trying to look confident, trying to look like all the other theater patrons, Wendy tucked her program under her arm and headed into the theater. She prayed that there would be empty seats.

She was one of the last people to enter the theater. The lights began to dim. Wendy panicked. She spotted a seat in the last row. It was awfully far back, but she should grab it before she got caught. Just as she was heading for it, she spotted two seats on the aisle quite close to the stage. Boldly, she scurried down the aisle and claimed one of the empty spots just as the curtain opened. It was the thirteenth row. How appropriate. For her thirteenth birthday.

She sat there terrified that an usher wielding a flashlight would find her, reveal her as an imposter and humiliate her. Her head buzzed, her heart banged and she was coated with sweat.

Minutes passed. Nothing happened. Everyone was watching the stage and no one came for the seats.

Eventually, the antics of the characters crept into her consciousness and reality melted away. Little by little, she began to unravel the tangled tale of the confused lovers. And, all the while, in the background of the forest set, the gleaming moon oversaw the fun.

Wendy gasped when the Queen of the Fairies, Titania, appeared high over the stage. Her arms were full of flowers, which she dropped tenderly on the lovers. Then she flew over the audience. Wendy had the distinct feeling that Titania was flying directly toward her. The next thing she knew, one of the white roses had landed right in her lap.

Wendy was thrilled that something so wonderful had happened on her birthday. Delighted, she followed the twists and turns of the play's silly plot until Puck delivered some of his final lines:

If we shadows have offended,
Think but this, and all is mended,

That you have but slumbered here
While these visions did appear.

That was it exactly, thought Wendy. The whole night had been like a dream. Everyone clapped and clapped. But, finally, the lights came up and Wendy started gathering her things. That was when she noticed the tiny rolled-up scroll of parchment nestled in the center petals of the rose. Curious, Wendy pulled it out. Carefully, she unrolled it.

Happy Birthday, Wendy dear.
    We're so glad you made it tonight. We knew you would. Now that you're of age, you are cordially invited to attend LATCH, the Lunar Arena of Transformation, Concentration and Hope. See you there.

Wendy stared and stared at this tiny little paper. What in the world did it mean? For the tenth time, Wendy re-read the note. It couldn't be a coincidence, a random prop that was thrown out to anyone in the audience. It was meant for her, on her birthday.

But what in the world could the Lunar Arena of Transformation, Concentration and Hope possibly be? She was invited to attend. But how did she get there? Where was it? When?

Wendy was not aware that she was the only one left in the audience or that the lights had been turned off. But suddenly her worst fear came true. The harsh beam of a flashlight blinded her. An usher glared at her accusingly.

"What are you doing here? You thought you were going to play one of those pranks and stay in here all night, didn't you? C'mon, you have to go." The irritated woman grabbed Wendy's arm and yanked her up.

"I just lost track of the time. I'm sorry," Wendy stuttered as the rose and note fell on the floor.

"Let go!" Wendy insisted as she lunged to the dark floor and felt around. Her hand closed over the note and a wave of relief flooded over her. Then she felt the rose. But as she reached for it, it snapped in two.

"Oh no, I broke it," Wendy said. "And it's my birthday."

Something about Wendy's genuine distress touched the usher. "All right, all right, my dear. I'm sorry I jumped to conclusions. Let me help you out of here."

Wendy carefully packed her program, note and rose into her bag.

"How lovely that you got a rose on your birthday. It's a nice touch, isn't it? The audience loves it." Firmly, the usher escorted Wendy to the exit door.

Wendy was more confused than ever. Titania must throw flowers every night. How did hers happen to have a note in it . . . addressed to her? Wendy was dying to ask the usher all these questions.

"Good night, dear. Happy Birthday." The usher opened the fire door.

"But . . ." The heavy door slammed in Wendy's face.

Somehow Wendy made it home. Not sure if she was going crazy—maybe she had had a nervous breakdown or a stroke . . . but, did thirteen-year-olds have them?—her trembling fingers reached into her bag and found it. By the light of the moon, the letters seemed to glow.

Happy Birthday, Wendy dear.

LATCH. The Lunar Arena of Transformation, Concentration and Hope. She wondered if she would ever sleep again.

Chapter Three

Wendy tossed and turned all night long. But in the morning she had no more answers to her questions. It was a hot summer day. She decided to take the boys to the Central Park Zoo. She had to do something to get her mind off last night.

The seals were having a blast in their cool water, but most of the animals were lethargic, curled up in the far corners of their areas, fast asleep.

"Come and get me," five-year-old Ralphie taunted, hoping for some reaction from the snow monkeys. They didn't even blink.

"They're boring," complained Joey.

"They're hot and sleepy," explained Wendy. "A lot of animals are most active at night."

"Can we come at night, then?" asked Ralphie.

"No, the zoo is closed at night," Wendy explained.

"That's dumb," Joey said.

Wendy tousled Joey's hair. "You're right. But that's just the way it is. Let's go to Sheep Meadow. You can run around there."

"Baa, baaaa," chimed in Eddie suddenly. He was just learning his animals and their noises. "See sheep!"

"I'm afraid the sheep are all gone, Eddie. They used to be there a long time ago."

"See sheep," Eddie insisted.

Finally, they were settled in a corner of Sheep Meadow. The boys were entranced by the vast expanse of grass. Ralphie had brought a ball and they all chased it, Eddie madly trying to keep up with his older brothers. They spotted a big white dog playing Frisbee with its owner.

Wendy took a deep breath and inhaled the fresh grassy smell. Had last night happened, or was it just a dream? And if it had happened, how did she find this LATCH?

Methodically, Wendy retraced every minute of the previous night. She had visited the very place that she had been left as a baby and it had been the beginning of the most amazing evening. She wasn't making things up. She had the napkin, the program, the rose and the note to prove it.

Well, she knew one thing. The word "lunar" referred to the moon. When the astronauts went on a lunar mission, they went to the moon. So LATCH must have something to do with the moon. But the note said, *See you there.* How was she supposed to go to the moon?

She figured that the way everything had unfolded last night, she was just supposed to wait. But Wendy couldn't stand it. What if there was something she was supposed to do? After all, if she hadn't planned her very first birthday celebration, she wouldn't have received the note in the first place.

Or would she? Wendy fingered the silver moon

around her neck. Her parents had left her with this necklace as a baby. She had always loved the moon, found comfort in the moon. It had to mean something.

Distantly, she registered peals of laughter and the pounding of feet. Before she could snap out of her reverie, four giant furry paws knocked her over and a big wet tongue started licking her face.

Wendy opened her eyes to see Ralphie, Joey and Eddie standing over her, laughing so hard they could barely stand up. A tall, distinguished-looking man appeared next to them.

"Luna!" he cried firmly. "Not now, Luna!" The man reached down and grabbed the dog's collar, pulling him away from Wendy. "I'm terribly sorry," the man said. "Sometimes he gets carried away. He was playing with the boys."

"I'm fine. I'm sure they enjoyed it. Thank you."

"It was our pleasure. Well, if you're sure you're okay. We must get going." And with that, the man and his dog walked off.

"That dog was cool," breathed Ralphie in awe.

"What was his name again?" asked Joey.

"Luna?" repeated Ralphie, clearly not understanding the name.

Goosebumps appeared on Wendy's skin despite the stifling, hot day. "Luna" was the Italian word for moon.

Chapter Four

A whole week had passed. Every day Wendy woke up hoping she would find out the next step for LATCH. But nothing happened.

Wendy did what she could. She went to the library. She read every word she could find on the moon, all its phases and stages. The Lunar Arena of Transformation was certainly an appropriate name because the moon transformed itself every twenty-seven days. In fact, the word "month" evolved from the word "moonth," because the concept of a month came from the moon's cycles. But reading about the moon wasn't making anything happen. Wendy felt like she was going to crawl right out of her skin if she had to wait a minute more.

Frustrated, she returned her book to the librarian, Ms. Davis.

"Are you all right, Wendy? You look a little tired." Ms. Davis asked kindly.

"I'm okay. I just can't find the answers that I'm looking for."

Ms. Davis narrowed her eyes. "Can I help?"

Ms. Davis' eyes seemed to bore into Wendy. How Wendy longed to tell her, to tell someone about LATCH, her birthday, the rose, the note, the whole thing. She had no one to talk to. Wendy hesitated.

"Have you ever heard of a place called LATCH?" Wendy finally whispered.

"LATCH?" Ms. Davis repeated, almost shouting. Wendy cringed. She sensed instinctively that talking about LATCH was wrong.

Wendy could hardly form a response. "I think it has something to do with the moon."

"Why don't you check the computer reference system. That has everything in it."

By sheer force of will, Wendy managed to smile. "Thank you, Ms. Davis. I'll do that," she replied politely, when what she really wanted to do was scream at the top of her lungs that for the past week she had checked the library computer, every phone book, every toll-free number that she could think of . . . and LATCH was nowhere to be found.

She had stood on her roof watching the moon grow smaller every night hoping that she would get a sign, a message, something. She had called the Library of Congress. She had waited and waited and waited. But, there was nothing, no information. And now, Wendy was quite certain that she had imagined the whole thing.

But maybe there was one last idea.

Her heart pounding, Wendy walked down the street to Shubert Alley. Somehow or other, she was going to get to the bottom of this. She'd get in the stage door if it killed her. She already had a story prepared. She planned to say she was visiting one of the actors. She had memorized the program and knew the names of everyone in the cast.

She spotted the marquis from the end of the street, but she couldn't read it. She walked closer. No, it couldn't be. She started running.

And then she stopped. There were no letters on the marquis. *A Midsummer Night's Dream* was gone. How could that be? It had only been a week since her birthday. She didn't remember any announcement saying that the play was closing. But it was gone—poof. Just like her parents. Just like LATCH. Just like all of Wendy's hopes.

Chapter Five

It was July 4. Another week had passed. Nothing. Nothing at all. The boys had wanted her to go to a holiday picnic with them, but Wendy didn't have the energy. She felt totally drained. Nothing was going to come of LATCH. Wendy had to accept it now.

She dragged herself to Central Park. Just to get out. She walked and walked until she came to Sheep Meadow. It looked peaceful and green. Wendy scanned the enormous lawn and was surprised to spot the big white dog, Luna, that she had seen two weeks ago. He was playing frisbee again with his owner.

Wendy tried to focus on her reading, but she found herself fascinated by the frisbee game. For a big dog, Luna was able to jump remarkably high. Wendy was mesmerized by the white dog and the white frisbee.

And then, the frisbee came right toward her. Panting, racing, the dog bounded in her direction, leaped up right in front of her and caught the flying disc in his mouth.

That was when it happened. Luna turned and looked straight at her and barked. The frisbee fell right into her lap. Close up, Wendy could see an astonishing thing. The frisbee wasn't plain white as she had thought. It had markings on it, circles and dark splotches. The more she stared at it, the more she realized that it looked just like the face of the moon. With a funny feeling in her stomach, she turned it over. There was a message on the back.

LATCH starts tonight. Bring your invitation and your ID.

For a moment, the world was a blur. And, then it all clicked into place. Finally, she'd received the missing piece of this torturous jigsaw puzzle. All the tension that had been building up for the last two weeks eased out of her body. Her waiting was over. Tonight was the beginning.

Her vision cleared and her brain seemed to be able to process what had happened. She reached for the frisbee to read it again, but it was gone. She looked up. The dog and the owner were gone. She stood up and shouted, "Luna, Luna." But, the people around her hardly paid any attention. She had so many questions to ask and no one to answer them.

For a long time Wendy sat on the lawn staring and thinking about where she was supposed to go, what she was supposed to do. She didn't think she should stay in the park. But where should she go? Or maybe it didn't matter. Maybe LATCH would find her wherever she was . . . just like the frisbee.

* * *

All the way home, Wendy had mulled over the words on the frisbee: *your invitation and your ID.* Back in her bedroom she reached for her basket on the top shelf of her closet and lifted it down. Gently, she held the miniature scroll that had been tucked in the rose. That had to be her invitation. But her ID? What could that be? She grabbed her school ID, her library card, and then she remembered the rose. That must be it. She stowed everything in her backpack.

She was ready.

Unfortunately, the sun was still blazing. She tried to read to distract herself, but she couldn't concentrate on the words. It seemed to take forever before the sun started to set. Suddenly, Wendy felt that she couldn't stay inside for one more second. She put on her backpack and climbed up the fire escape to the roof.

Another family from the building was having a Fourth of July barbecue on the roof. Wendy settled down in her favorite spot by the chimney and searched for the moon. She couldn't find it.

A crashing noise filled the air and a ball of exploding lights appeared over the East River. The fireworks had begun. Wendy stared at the fireworks, lost in their spell.

"Hi, I'm Pedro." Seeming to appear out of nowhere, a slight, dark-haired boy was inches from Wendy's face, grinning as if he knew something that she didn't. His pearly teeth seemed to glow in the dark. His hair was cut at all angles and stuck up from his head.

Wendy jumped. "You scared me. I thought I was alone."

"Not anymore," he teased. "I've been planning to meet you for a long time, Wendy."

"How do you know my name?"

Pedro shrugged. "I guess I've heard my aunt and uncle mention it." He motioned to the family having the barbecue.

"But I don't know them."

"Well, they live in your building. They must have heard your name."

Wendy was very skeptical. No one knew her. But Pedro kept smiling. He really seemed very friendly and harmless. Anyway, he was inches shorter and pounds lighter than her. No real threat. She couldn't help smiling back.

Something in the sky caught Pedro's eye. "Oh, look, you can just see the new moon disappearing."

Wendy turned. A huge bouquet of fireworks ignited the sky. Ever so faintly on the horizon, Wendy could make out the palest suggestion of the moon. "Just barely."

He smiled his infectious grin at her again. "That's because the only light hitting the side of the moon that we're seeing is coming from the earth."

"You know a lot about the moon."

"A little. See you around." Pedro walked away with a wave of his hand.

Wendy felt vaguely unsettled by Pedro's appearance. But there was something very likeable about him. Eventually the family left and Wendy felt uncomfortable all alone on the roof. She climbed back to her room knowing she would never be able to sleep.

Chapter Six

Hour after hour ticked by. Wendy stared at the moonless sky. Then she heard something, a soft tapping at her window. Wendy sat up in bed. Someone was on her fire escape. His face was pressed against the glass. Just as Wendy was opening her mouth to scream, she recognized him. It was Pedro.

He was smiling and beckoning her to open the window. For some reason, Wendy didn't think twice. She flipped open the lock.

Pedro's eyes twinkled. "I've come to take you to LATCH. I'm your buddy. Are you ready?"

Wendy's eyes widened. LATCH! He knew about LATCH. A thousand questions raced through her mind. Why hadn't he mentioned it earlier? What was LATCH? How did they find her? Trying not to be flustered, she nodded, bit her lip to keep from babbling, and slipped on her backpack.

He held his hand out to her through the open window. As if in slow motion . . . somehow knowing that her life was never going to be the same . . . Wendy placed her hand in his.

The next moments were a blur. And then, it seemed that she was no longer in her room or even on the fire escape. She was somewhere else entirely. Still holding her hand, Pedro was leading her into a very dark room with no windows. At the side of the room was a short corridor with big gray doors.

"We need your invitation and ID," Pedro explained.

Wendy felt her legs go to jelly. She hoped she had the right things. She pulled out the tiny scroll. Pedro nodded. "Good, now the ID."

"I'm not sure . . . ," Wendy mumbled frantically as she searched for the rose.

Gently, Pedro turned her to face the doors. He adjusted her shoulders so that she was positioned just so, and suddenly her moon necklace reflected a tiny crescent shape on the door. As it did, a crescent shaped keyhole appeared, aligned with the reflection from her necklace, and the door swung open.

Wendy laughed with relief and amazement. She had always had her ID. Her parents had given her ID to her when she was a newborn. She was meant to be here.

Pedro pulled his own crescent moon from under his shirt. "See, I have a moon key, too," he explained. "We all do. It grants you access to LATCH." He motioned Wendy to enter.

Solemnly, Wendy walked through the doors . . . onto the moon. Everywhere she looked was the luminescent, shadowy, familiar face of the moon. Where was she? Was she really on the moon?

Gradually, she realized that she was in a large round room with a domed ceiling. In the center of the room was a low, circular platform, like a stage, surrounded by tiers of seats.

"Welcome to LATCH," Pedro said. "Let's get a seat."

"Hey, Helena!" Pedro called out as he spotted someone. The most breathtakingly beautiful blonde turned around. The gorgeous girl stood up and motioned for Pedro and Wendy to come join her.

Wendy felt self-conscious and awkward. Just as they reached Helena, Wendy stumbled and pitched forward onto the lap of the boy sitting next to Helena. Her head hit him in the stomach.

"You big oaf. Get off me." The angry boy grabbed handfuls of Wendy's hair and yanked her away from him.

"I'm sorry," Wendy mumbled, sensing that the boy had already judged her to be lower than a clod of mud.

Then Helena's gentle hands were steadying her, helping her to get her balance. Wendy had the strongest sense that she had seen Helena before.

"There was no reason to react like that, Phillip. She just tripped." Helena sighed in exasperation. "By the way, this is my cousin . . . and buddy . . . ," she added reluctantly, "Phillip."

Phillip jumped up and thrust out his hand importantly. "Phillip Huntington, the Fourth, of Park Avenue and Tuxedo Park, at your service."

Pedro's eyes danced with mischief. "Hey, Phil, *que pasa?*" Pedro raised his hand, and before Phillip could figure out what was happening, slapped his hand in a high five. Phillip looked truly appalled.

"I'm Pedro and this is Wendy Hilton," Pedro added.

Phillip's eyebrows arched skeptically. "Wendy Hilton

as in the Hiltons of Palm Beach?" Phillip's eyes slid over Wendy's hand-me-down clothing.

Wendy didn't get mad easily, but Phillip was obnoxious. If he was an example of the people at LATCH, Wendy wasn't at all sure that she wanted to be there. She drew herself up. "I don't know the Hiltons of Palm Beach. I'm the Wendy Hilton . . . of 104th Street."

Phillip all but snickered, and whispered audibly to Helena, "Who are these two, the scholarship group?"

Helena looked fed up. "Enough, Phillip."

Pedro slid into the seat next to Helena and Wendy sat next to him—as far as she could get from Phillip. The lights were suddenly dimmed and an eerie musical sound filled the room. A powerful blue spotlight illuminated the center circle of the room as the floor moved and a woman rose up through the opening.

"Welcome to the Lunar Arena of Transformation, Concentration and Hope." Not a whisper sounded. The woman's voice was so beautiful, lush and hypnotic. "Some of you may have heard of LATCH before. But, for most of you, this evening is a surprise."

The woman smiled and Wendy gasped. She knew her. She was the woman who had played Titania. She was sure of it. What kind of force was at work here? Maybe, that performance of *A Midsummer Night's Dream* had been performed just for her. But that was crazy. Wendy forced herself to concentrate on what Titania was saying.

"As you have probably guessed, an invitation to LATCH is a privilege. The reasons you have been chosen may seem mysterious, just as the moon is. . . ."

"I would say so." Phillip's voice carried as he leaned forward to peer pointedly at Wendy.

"I can tell you that you have been chosen, not for what you are . . . but for what you can be. That is the goal of LATCH—to push you, to challenge you, to offer you opportunities to fulfill your potential.

"But I must warn you. The most important thing is to keep your mind completely open. What seems to be and what is . . . can be two entirely different things. What you want to be and what you have the potential to be can also be two completely different things. Like the moon, we are all composed of many traits, many personalities. During the course of LATCH's five phases, you will be able to explore many of them."

Then a strange thing happened. Titania seemed to twirl around and an older man with silver streaks in his hair was standing in her place. The entire group gasped.

"Good evening." The man winked at them. "Nice trick, eh? I am Petavius. But everyone calls me Pet. The moon is the driving force of LATCH. Its constancy, its changeability, its allure have been inspiring poets, philosophers, scientists and dreamers for centuries. All our activities take place by the light of the moon."

Wendy put her hand up to her mouth to stifle her gasp. She recognized him, too. He was the man in Sheep Meadow with the dog, Luna.

Wendy forced herself to concentrate on Pet's words, "We have done our best to identify the best people for LATCH. However, as in all things in life, there is a margin for error. That is why we refer to you as candidates. There are three . . . I hate to call them tests because at LATCH we have no homework or tests . . . shall we call them . . . revelations . . . through which we know who is right for LATCH and you learn if LATCH is right for you."

Phillip whispered to Helena. "What a joke. Our family has been part of LATCH for generations. I'm surprised they just don't let me skip this part."

"No one gets to skip this part, Phillip," Helena whispered back. "Not even you."

Wendy felt a little queasy. What if the revelations disclosed the fact that she did not belong here? She touched the cool, curved surface of her necklace. She reminded herself that her parents had left her with the necklace. It was the key to LATCH. She must belong here. She wanted to belong somewhere so badly.

"There is no reason to be nervous. LATCH is not about passing or failing. The revelations only reveal the truth. However, LATCH is not the best place for everyone. It is better for all of us to find that out right away." Pet finished and seemed to look directly at Wendy. Wendy's stomach flipped. Then, before she knew what was happening, the eerie music was playing again and Pet had disappeared.

Pedro looked at Wendy's glazed eyes and laughed sympathetically. "I know, it's overwhelming. I'm sure you have a thousand questions. I'll answer as many as I'm allowed to."

"What does that mean?" Wendy asked a little indignantly. She was tired of so little information.

"The principal philosophy of LATCH is for the participants to understand the key concepts through their own experience. We have to discover them for ourselves." Pedro shrugged.

Frankly, it all made Wendy quite nervous. It worried her that she wouldn't be able to figure out what she was supposed to do without some guidance. But she kept quiet.

Pedro and Wendy moved back to the refreshment tables. The punch bowl was filled with a swirling liquid that glowed as if it were alive.

Pedro watched Wendy's face. "That's Sea of Nectar Punch. Pretty cool, isn't it?"

"It looks . . . bewitched," stuttered Wendy. "Can you really drink it?"

Pedro poured her a cup. The luminescent liquid twinkled in the cut glass, sometimes appearing blue, sometimes white, emanating a rainbow sheen. "Try it."

Wendy sipped it. Oh my. It was delicious.

"What does it taste like?" Pedro asked.

Wendy was confused. "You know. You've had it before."

"How would you describe it?" Pedro pressed.

Wendy closed her eyes. "Like ripe strawberries, still warm from the sun, that you've just picked and popped into your mouth. I did that once on a farm trip for school."

"For me, it's like my favorite Easter egg, chocolate and hazelnut, but you can drink it." Wendy's eyes widened. Pedro explained, "Sea of Nectar Punch tastes different to everyone."

Phillip and Helena joined them in time to hear Pedro's remark. "I would have described it as the sublime white chocolate truffles that I have enjoyed many times at the baron's chateau on Lake Geneva, in Switzerland," Phillip said.

Helena smiled. "Phillip, stop name dropping."

Wendy stared at the other girl. She was so breathtakingly beautiful. It was then that Wendy figured it out. She had seen Helena before on the cover of

Glamour and *Cosmopolitan*. She was a top fashion model known only as H.

Helena caught her eye and made a funny face. "You're right. You've seen me before. The modeling is part of my self-projection work for LATCH. You'll see. Pretty amazing, isn't it?"

"No, it's not amazing at all," responded Wendy. "You're stunning."

Helena burst out laughing. "It's all because of LATCH. I certainly didn't believe that before I started here. I'll show you some old pictures of me some-time. You'll see."

Helena turned away to speak to someone else and Wendy stood there baffled. She was in the wrong place if she was ever supposed to convince people that she was beautiful.

And then she sensed that someone had come up behind her. She spun around to find Petavius smiling at her.

"So glad you could make it," he said warmly.

Wendy was practically speechless. "I wouldn't have missed it. These last two weeks have seemed endless."

Pet laughed. "Sorry about that. I'm afraid that you did seem a little droopy in the park. It's the moon, you know. We always distribute the invitations on the day of a full moon. It has the most powerful magic. But LATCH always starts with the new moon. Beginnings, of course. That creates the delay."

That was it. Her birthday had been on the full moon. And now, it was a new moon. "Boy, I wish you could indicate that on the invitation. I thought I was going to lose my mind."

"We are introducing many concepts here. They start with trust and confidence and accepting truths without full information. Letting go and accepting."

"I'm afraid I failed that part," Wendy admitted with chagrin.

Pet wagged his finger. "Didn't you listen to my opening remarks? No one passes or fails here. You'll be fine." And with a reassuring smile, Petavius seemed to melt into the crowd and vanish.

Wendy's eyes fluttered open as she heard the birds chirping. She felt relaxed and hopeful for the first time in weeks. All because of LATCH. It was amazing that she could have been up all night and feel so great. How had she gotten home? The last thing she remembered was talking to Petavius. And now it was six o'clock in the morning. She was lying in her bed in the same clothes that she had worn last night. It was as if it had never happened.

Then a horrible sinking feeling washed over her. Of course, that was it. It had all been a dream. Her desperate mind had made up the whole thing. She had thought that she was awake all night, but she had obviously fallen asleep.

She grew furious with herself. She was such a baby, always believing in fairy tales, waiting for something magical to change her life. A deep sadness filled her. LATCH didn't exist. Her necklace was just a necklace, not a moon key. She had dreamed the whole thing.

She lay there staring at the ceiling. She realized that she was being ridiculous. She had made a vow on her birthday. And she would keep it. No more moping around. She flipped the covers off of her, and as she did, she noticed something on her shirt. It looked like a few drops of Sea of Nectar Punch. She must be imagining things again.

Chapter Seven

Wendy moved through the day, her mind a total jumble. Was LATCH real or not? She dreaded going to bed and put it off as long as she could, truly afraid of waiting for something that might not happen. She opened her book, promising herself that she would not fall asleep.

She heard a noise and bolted up in bed. Someone was in her room. Ready to fight, she whipped around to face the intruder. Pedro stood by the window, wearing his impish grin.

"Are you trying to scare me to death?"

Pedro pressed a finger to to his lips and shook his head. Without a word, he led her out of the window, up the fire escape, and onto the roof.

"*Buenos nochos,*" Pedro said softly. "Do you have any questions?"

"Only about a thousand," Wendy smiled on. "I didn't find out nearly enough last night. When does LATCH meet? What am I supposed to do? How do I know what is going on?"

"The first thing you have to do is *trust*," Pedro replied. "Even when it's cloudy, you don't worry that the moon is up in the sky. You know it's there behind the clouds. Well, the same is true for LATCH. LATCH is as constant as the moon, always there, ever-changing."

Wendy felt more confused than ever. "Are we going to LATCH tonight?" She decided to cut to the chase and go for a simple yes or no answer.

Pedro laughed. "Yes, we are. But not together."

The minute Pedro said "yes," Wendy breathed a sigh of relief. It took a few seconds for the rest of his response to get through to her brain. "I thought you were my buddy."

"I am. But you must go through the revelations on your own. That's the whole point."

Wendy was scared. "Can't you tell me what to expect? What kind of a buddy are you?"

"The revelations are as simple as looking into a mirror and seeing what is there. How difficult is that?"

Wendy gestured ruefully at her lumpy body. "Looking in the mirror has never been one of my favorite activities."

Very gently and seriously Pedro said, "Maybe you're not looking deeply enough. LATCH will help open your eyes. That's the biggest tip I can give you. Trust that the power that is in you is more than enough, or you wouldn't have been chosen for LATCH."

Wendy fingered her necklace. "But I wasn't chosen. It's because of my parents."

Pedro raised his chocolate brown eyes to meet hers. "Just having a connection is not enough. Let me assure you. You have been chosen."

A thrill ran through Wendy. Maybe there was

something special inside her after all. Before she could think about what it all meant, a bell off in the distance started to toll midnight. She heard a rushing in her ears and the next thing she knew, Pedro was gone and she was standing somewhere in the darkness with the ringing right over her head.

She looked up and two bronze monkeys were hitting a bell with hammers while six animals rotated underneath and played "Three Blind Mice." It was so dark. Where in the world was she?

Wendy had a vague feeling that she had seen these animals before. And then it came to her. She was at the Delacorte Clock in Central Park right by the Children's Zoo. She had walked by the bronze monkeys recently with the boys.

The monkeys hit the bell for the fourth time and the music stopped. "Good evening," boomed a gravelly voice. Wendy whirled around, feeling a little dizzy as she caught sight of the life-sized bronze bear statue stepping out of its alcove in the brick wall opposite the clock.

It occurred to Wendy that she should feel afraid. But everything was so odd that she didn't have time to feel frightened until someone came running from the shadows and bashed into her.

"Ouch!" she yelled as her foot got crushed.

"You were in my way, you cow!" a voice retorted accusingly.

Wendy turned to find herself face-to-face with Phillip.

"I should have known that we'd be in the same group," Phillip said in disgust.

"Same group?" Wendy murmured, as she noticed for the first time that there was a cluster of kids her age gathered around.

"Yes, of course, you dolt. Don't you know anything? The revelations are done in groups. Naturally, we're together. Huntington and Hilton."

"Welcome to your first session at LATCH," the bear said. "We've broken our new candidates into four groups by the alphabet. The eight of you are in the Humorum Group. The other three groups are Atlas, Olbers and Theophilus. All named from the moon, of course. I'm sure that you have a lot of questions. But bear with me—get it, *bear* with me," he repeated with a chuckle, "and see if you can discover the answers on your own."

The more the bear talked, the more certain Wendy was that she recognized the bear's voice. It had to be Petavius. Somehow, he had changed his form.

She glanced around and spotted a tiny girl standing as still as a rock in the deep shadows. She seemed very frightened. "Hello. I'm Wendy Hilton," Wendy said gently.

The girl, who barely reached Wendy's armpit, raised her head. Her deep blue-black eyes glinted in the evening light, but she said nothing.

"What's your name?" Wendy pressed, sensing that the girl was too terrified to speak.

"April Moon." Her voice was so soft that Wendy wasn't sure if the girl was speaking or if the wind was blowing.

"April who?" Wendy asked.

"April Moon," the girl repeated. And then suddenly, her delicate face broke into an infectious grin. "Pretty good name for LATCH, huh?"

Wendy was so startled by the change in the girl's demeanor that she laughed out loud. "I'd say."

April spoke with a subtle accent. Her hair was

poker straight, shiny black, cut in bangs. "Do you know anything about LATCH?" she asked.

"Not really," admitted Wendy.

April shrugged nonchalantly. "Neither do I. I guess we'll figure it out as we go along. We better follow him." April pointed to the bear, who was moving away.

Wendy was quickly revising her opinion of this tiny dynamo. April didn't seem intimidated by the situation at all.

"Aren't you nervous?" Wendy asked April.

April's eyes twinkled. "As far as I know, I'm still fast asleep in my bed on Grand Street and this is all a dream—a weird, fun dream. What terrible thing can possibly happen while we're safe asleep in bed?" April giggled.

Wendy wasn't as convinced that she was safe asleep in bed. But if April could look at their situation that way, so could she!

They were walking along behind the bear when they heard a great flapping sound. Eight enormous eagles, each at least six feet tall, landed right in front of them. They had piercing eyes and menacing, curved beaks. They seemed to be made of stone, but they were moving.

"Good evening, Royal Guards." The bear nodded his head deferentially to the giant birds of prey.

"Good evening. We have come to escort you to your first revelation," the head eagle announced.

"Very good," the bear said, nodding.

Before Wendy knew what was happening, an eagle appeared at her side, stretched out the talons of his powerful feet, hopped in the air and picked her up by the back of her clothing.

Before Wendy could react, she was sailing about fifty feet over the zoo. All too quickly, she was set down as gently as she had been picked up.

"Wasn't that great?" April bounded over to Wendy, obviously thrilled by her sky ride. "My eagle's name was Everest. What was yours?"

Wendy had no idea. She had been too frightened to even think of talking to her eagle. Wendy looked around and was shocked again. Although she had never observed the exhibit from this perspective, she realized that they were standing on the rocky island in the middle of the sea lion exhibit.

The bear stood in front of them. "So, who would like to be first?" he asked.

"I'll go." In a flash, Phillip stripped off his outer clothes, revealing a bathing suit. Clearly, he had been prepared for this activity. Phillip held up his hand and the three sea lions jumped out of the water. Wendy could have sworn that he had treats for them. Wasn't that cheating?

With no further instruction, Phillip did a perfect dive into the tank and effortlessly swam a powerful circle around the tank with the sea lions beside him. Then he climbed up on the rocks. The rest of the group clapped and Phillip bowed. It was obvious that he loved being the star.

After Phillip, each LATCH candidate took turns swimming around the tank with varying degrees of expertise. Wendy's heart thumped in her chest. She couldn't do this. She was afraid of the sea lions and terrified of the water.

Finally, only April and Wendy were left. "I can't swim," Wendy whispered frantically.

April volunteered to go next and flashed Wendy a look. Wendy expected the other girl to undress, but

April jumped into the water with her clothes on. She didn't float to the top to breathe or stroke with her arms like everyone else had. She put her hands at her sides and zoomed off under the water just like the sea lions.

All the kids gasped in surprise and delight. April had become a sea lion. Wendy wondered how this was possible, but, nothing made much sense at LATCH. Wendy snuck a peak at the bear. He seemed to be smiling. Then Wendy noticed Phillip's face. It was ugly and contorted with jealousy. It was clear he didn't care for being one-upped.

As Wendy was observing all this, April splashed out of the water and grabbed her hand. "Let's go, it's a blast!"

Wendy jerked back. "I can't."

"Yes, you can," insisted April. She got right up next to Wendy's ear. "Close your eyes and believe that you're a sea lion."

Wendy took a deep breath and was yanked into the tank. Terrified, she swallowed a mouthful of water and choked. She kicked up to the surface frantically, coughing and spitting out water. "I can't," she sobbed.

"Trust me." April squeezed Wendy's hand. Just then Wendy caught a glimpse of Phillip's mocking face. With all her might, Wendy tried to imagine being a smooth, sleek sea lion flowing with the water.

After a minute, she must have succeeded, at least a little, because she could feel herself moving. And then Wendy got up the courage to open her eyes. Her hand was no longer in April's, but holding onto the flipper of one of the sea lions. Startled, she let go of the flipper. Incredibly, she continued moving through the tank.

Finally, she pulled herself out of the water. April started clapping and then everyone else joined in, except Phillip. "See, you did it on your own," April said.

Wendy wasn't at all sure that was true.

"Now we must move on," announced the bear. In a blur, Wendy was aware that her clothes were not even wet. April looked dry, too. How could that be?

The clock started chiming. One . . . two . . . three. . . . Had they really been with the sea lions for three hours? Wendy wondered when they would finish.

"Thank you so much," Wendy whispered to April. "I'm deathly afraid of the water. I've never learned to swim."

April grinned. "Neither have I."

Wendy couldn't believe her ears. "But you were a natural."

April nodded matter-of-factly. "I was a sea lion. Weren't they nice? Seaweed was the one who escorted you around."

"How do you know their names?" asked Wendy.

"I talked to them, didn't you?" asked April.

"Talked to them?"

"Their names are Seaweed, Scooter, and believe it or not, April, just like me!"

Wendy's head was spinning. That was when she saw the eagles. At the end of each of the four paths leading from the sea lion tank were two six-foot carved stone eagle statues. The same eagles who had been flying a very little while ago.

"You cheated!" accused a biting voice coming from behind them.

April casually turned around. "I don't think we're the cheaters, Huntie. We didn't come with treats for the sea lions, or bathing suits under our clothes. I bet you have a cheat sheet for every revelation at

LATCH. Must take some of the fun out of it to be so privileged."

Phillip ignored April's reply and reached out to touch her shirt. "Your clothes aren't even wet. That's impossible. How'd you do it? Some kind of ancient Eastern magic?"

April's lips curved into a Mona Lisa smile. "I'll never tell."

"You'll never get away with it. I'll see to it," he threatened.

April's feathery voice grew somehow ominous. "Nice learning about your real self, Huntie. I guess that's what the revelations are all about." And with that April walked away with Wendy.

Chapter Eight

The bear stopped by another rocky island surrounded by water: the snow monkey exhibit. Unlike
the day last week when the monkeys had been sleeping, they were up and alert. Wendy wished that Ralphie could see them now.

The bear was talking.

"Doesn't he sound like Petavius?" Wendy whispered to April.

April nodded. "You're right."

"Did you know that Petavius is the name of one of
the biggest craters on the moon?" Wendy couldn't
resist showing off her knowledge. "I did a lot of re-
search on the moon when I first got my invitation,"
Wendy continued, then stopped. The bear was staring at her.

"Wendy Hilton, why don't you go first this time,"
he suggested.

With Phillip snickering at her, Wendy tried to look
confident. The bear motioned for her to climb the
fence, which posed no problem. Wendy wasn't sure

how to navigate the moat of water on the other side, though. As she contemplated trying to swim again, a snow monkey pushed a hanging vine over to her.

Without thinking, Wendy grabbed the vine and swung across the moat, landing next to the three monkeys. They sat staring at her with their rose-colored faces and brown coats. Because they were a lot smaller than she was, Wendy didn't feel in any physical danger. But she didn't have a clue what she was supposed to do.

Then she reminded herself of Pedro's words. She wasn't supposed to *do* anything. This was not a test, it was a revelation. All of a sudden, Wendy knew who these three monkeys reminded her of and what she wanted to do. She grabbed a handful of ripe berries and playfully threw them at the animals.

In a flash, the monkeys understood the game. They wanted to play too. Wendy was soon covered with splattered berry stains. Scrambling all over the island, Wendy and the three monkeys had a grand time. From tug-of-war with a fallen vine to king of the castle as they all tried to stand on the peak of the rock, the monkeys seemed to accept Wendy as one of their own.

When Wendy's turn was over, April gave her a thumbs-up. "You were a natural at that. You must have been a snow monkey in another life."

"The monkeys looked exactly like my foster brothers when they get bored. So I did what I do with the boys—I played with them."

April nodded. "You seemed to understand them."

Wendy thought about April's comment as she watched the other kids. She did seem to understand their silliness better than anyone else.

Finally, it was Phillip's turn. From the minute he joined the monkeys he was stiff and uncomfortable. The monkeys didn't seem to like him. Phillip climbed to the top of the island to show his supremacy. One by one, the monkeys surrounded him and began to tease him. One pinched him. One untied his shoes.

"Hey, stop that," Phillip shouted when the third monkey stole a small index card from his pocket. The monkey ignored him and scampered down the peak. Just as the monkey was about to drop the card in the moat, Phillip lunged for it, lost his balance and fell into the water. When he looked back, the monkey was calmly chewing the card.

Angry, Phillip wouldn't give up. He grabbed the monkey and tried to get the card out of his mouth. The other monkeys didn't like that. They circled Phillip, making strange noises and baring their teeth.

Instantly, the bear took charge, calming the monkeys and guiding Phillip off the island.

April said, "Mr. Huntington the Fourth just went up in flames and lost his cheat sheet. Do you think he learned anything? Like you shouldn't lord it over people . . . or animals?"

Wendy shrugged, "I doubt it."

Once again, Pet was on the move. The bells rang. Wendy counted along, anticipating four rings. But they only rang once.

"That's weird," Wendy said. "The last time they rang three times, after the sea lions."

"I thought so, too," April replied. "But maybe we didn't hear right."

Pet stopped again. The night was very black now, actually darker than it had been at the sea lion exhibit. All Wendy could see in the darkness were huge white shapes, glowing like ghosts. A shiver went up her spine. They stood outside the polar bear exhibit. Polar bears were a completely different ball game from cute little snow monkeys.

April didn't seem to share Wendy's hesitation. In fact, she volunteered to go first. One of the eagles appeared to fly her over the moat. The bears were sleeping. April moved up to them and petted them gently. One of the bears opened his eyes and then went back to sleep. They seemed harmless.

Wendy began to breathe more deeply. Maybe this revelation wouldn't be so bad. One by one, the other students took their turns. The bears were dead to the world. Soon only Wendy and Phillip were left.

"Well, it looks like a quiet night," Petavius commented, looking a little disappointed.

"I'll go now," volunteered Phillip. Phillip entered the arctic region. But instead of going to the sleeping bears, he climbed to the other side where a small arctic fox was sleeping. The fox was much more high strung than the bears. He perked up his ears and opened his eyes. Soon Phillip was throwing a stick to him like a dog. For the next few minutes, Phillip played with the fox, gradually leading him back to the area where the bears were sleeping.

"All right, that's enough," called Pet. "We're running out of time."

Wendy thought that was curious. Did their LATCH session have a specific ending time?

"Very well, has everybody gone?" asked Pet.

For a split second, Wendy thought that if she didn't speak up, maybe she'd slip by without having to go in with the polar bears.

"I don't think Wendy has gone . . . ," came a helpful voice, ever so casually. Of course, it was Phillip.

Remembering photos she had seen of polar bears tearing apart their prey, Wendy tried not to be afraid when the eagle deposited her in the exhibit. The arctic fox was jumping around, eager to play some more. Wendy had to admit that he was adorable, not much bigger than a cat, with fluffy white fur and big pointy ears.

She was about to throw the stick to the fox when something happened. Suddenly, one of the polar bears woke up with a growl.

Wendy panicked and began to scramble in the opposite direction. However, the fox was just a few feet from the growling animal. The next thing Wendy knew, the aggravated bear lunged at the fox. Wendy watched paralyzed. Then, she jumped up and started making crazy noises. She couldn't stand by while the cute little fox got attacked by the bear.

The bear, more irritated than ever, looked at Wendy, but then he turned back to the fox, who was frozen in a rocky corner. Impulsively, Wendy threw the stick at the bear. It glanced off the soft part of his nose. The bear roared—the loudest, most outraged roar Wendy had ever heard. And then, faster than Wendy could imagine for an animal of his size, the enormous polar bear came barreling toward her.

Wendy heard a blaring noise like a siren and then everything went black.

Slowly, Wendy opened her eyes. A shadowy circle of faces looked down on her.

"Sorry, my dear. Sometimes, the revelations are a little more dramatic than we intend them to be. How are you feeling?" Pet murmured.

It was all coming back to her. "I'm OK. . . ."

"You were very brave," said Pet. "I think we all learned a lot tonight."

April helped Wendy to stand up. "You fainted and the eagle snatched you out of there."

Wendy couldn't believe that she had been so frightened that she had fainted. "What a wimp. . . ."

April was shocked at Wendy's words. "You were wonderful protecting the fox. *He* threw a stone at the bear!"

"What?" Wendy did not understand.

"*Phillip!* He's the one who set you up!" April was livid.

"Unfortunately, Pet didn't see him. But, in the end, Phillip's whole stupid plan backfired and you ended up the hero," April finished dramatically.

"He could have gotten me killed. What is with him?" Wendy asked softly, just as the bells sounded in the distance. *Bong, bong, bong, bong . . .*

Wendy's eyes fluttered open. Where was April? Then she spotted her book lying open next to her. The light was still on. She must have dozed off while she was reading before Pedro came.

. . . *Bong, bong, bong, bong, bong, bong, bong, bong.* Wendy counted twelve rings in all. How could that be? Her digital clock said 12:00, too.

Her clock must have stopped. She had specifically heard the bells chime three times after they visited the sea lions. It had to be much later now, at least four or five o'clock in the morning.

But the sky was still pitch dark. She looked at her wrist watch. It also said 12:00. The reality of her situation was undeniable. It was midnight. But how could she have dozed off for a split second and had such an elaborate dream? So much had happened. It was as if time had gone backwards and it was earlier in the evening than it had been hours ago. But that was crazy.

On top of everything, she was physically exhausted, as if she had been up for hours, swimming and climbing rocks. But here she was under her sheet. Everything indicated that she had never left her bed. April had to be right. It was all a dream, including April. It was the only explanation for why no time had passed.

It was all too much to think about. Wendy buried her head under her pillow and promptly fell asleep.

Chapter Nine

"What happened to your clothes?" giggled Joey the next morning. "They look like they have chicken pox."

Wendy looked down. She was still wearing the jeans and T-shirt that she had fallen asleep in last night. She hadn't noticed when she jumped out of bed, but they had purple splotches on them . . . the same color as the berries the snow monkeys had pelted her with.

Wendy's face flushed as bright as the stains on her clothes. Wasn't this proof? It couldn't have been a dream. April was wrong. "Oh, I guess I spilled something."

"Then, why are you smiling?" Joey asked.

Wendy got the three boys to watch TV while she searched for a telephone book. She flipped it open to the Ms.

Boy, there were a lot of Moons in Manhattan. She ran down the columns, racking her brain for some other clue. Then it came to her. April had mentioned that she lived on Grand Street. Wendy's eyes scanned the list. Bingo. She prayed that this was the right number. She had to find April, to find out if she was real. She dialed the number.

"Hi." A female voice answered the phone with a clipped greeting.

"Hello. I'm Wendy Hilton. Is April there, April Moon?"

There was a silence and then a burst of words. Unfortunately, they were in a language that Wendy didn't understand. The phone was put down and Wendy waited, holding her breath.

"Wendy, is that you?" April sounded astonished.

"You are real! See, we're not crazy, and I don't think that LATCH is just a dream!" Wendy blurted out with delight.

"Why do you say that?"

"Because my clothes are covered with purple splotches, the same color as the berries from the snow monkeys."

April paused, as if she was thinking hard. "Tell me everything you remember from your dream."

Wendy described the events of the previous night: the bear, Phillip, all the animals.

April sucked in a deep breath of air. "What was the name of my eagle?"

"Everest," Wendy replied confidently. "You see, either we, two total strangers, had the exact same fantastical dream, or it must have really happened."

"But how do you explain the time? When I woke up after my dream, it was exactly midnight. No time had passed at all," April insisted.

"That's exactly what happened to me. I've been racking my brain all night to figure it out. I can't remember how many times the bells rang when we arrived at the zoo, do you?"

"No, there was too much happening."

"Right. But I am pretty sure that they rang three times after the sea lions and once after the snow monkeys. It was midnight when we arrived back in our rooms." Wendy took a deep breath. "What if time goes *backwards* at LATCH?"

"That's nuts," April scoffed.

"I know it seems like that. But, it's the only theory that works. Next time, we just have to pay attention to the time. What if it's 4:00 A.M. when we arrive and then time goes backwards until it's midnight? At the stroke of midnight we return home. So, we still have plenty of time to rest. Didn't you feel like you got a full night's sleep?"

"I guess," April finally admitted.

"I think it's moon magic," whispered Wendy. "It doesn't have to make sense."

"What's weird is that some of LATCH is so real. I've been to the Children's Zoo before. And I think the first night took place at the planetarium in the Museum of Natural History. My class went there once," April said.

"I've never been there, but it seemed like a real place," Wendy agreed. "That's it, exactly. LATCH is sort of like . . . real magic."

April was quiet. "When do you think we'll go again?"

"That's the part I hate—waiting around, not knowing. Thank goodness we can call each other. Is there any chance we could get together during the day sometime?" Wendy asked.

"I don't know. My parents are old-world Korean, very protective."

"Is that the language you speak, Korean?"

"Yes. I'll have to see if I can work something out. I'll contact you, but I have to go now to help out in our dry cleaners," April said.

Wendy hung up, lost in her thoughts.

"You're smiling again," Joey said, startling Wendy.

"Yes," Wendy acknowledged as she gave Joey an impulsive hug. She had real magic and her first real friend.

Chapter Ten

That night Wendy couldn't wait to go to bed, but she dreaded it at the same time. It would be so exciting if there was another LATCH activity and such a letdown if nothing happened. At 11:00 P.M. she lay in bed trying to concentrate on her book. She had an hour to kill before midnight.

A knock at the window made her jump. *Yes!* Pedro was there. This time, Wendy didn't say a word until they were on the roof. "You're early. I'm so glad you're here," she bubbled. "Where are we going tonight?"

"Whoa, whoa," Pedro laughed at her enthusiasm.

"I can't stop thinking about LATCH." Wendy lowered her voice to a whisper. "I called April today, because I had to talk about LATCH with someone." Wendy's face grew ashen. "Are we allowed to do that? Oh, please don't tell Petavius if I wasn't supposed to contact April. . . ."

Pedro cut her off. "Don't worry. You can be friends

with other people from LATCH, and you can talk about LATCH all you want. Only someone who's experienced it would believe your stories. You actually participated and you're probably not sure if it was a dream or not."

"How did you know?" Wendy asked. "I thought something was wrong with me."

"We all feel the same way. In fact, I'm not sure that any of us are ever completely convinced that it's not all a dream. After all, the moon is the mother of dreams."

"So where are we going tonight?" Wendy asked eagerly.

"There are no activities tonight. Anyhow, it's too early. Surely you've figured that out by now," Pedro replied.

Wendy's disappointment was quickly overcome by her pride in her theory about LATCH time. "Well, it seems like time goes backwards at LATCH. When the clock strikes midnight, LATCH begins. But when we get there it's really 4:00 A.M. and time moves in reverse until it's midnight again and we're home in bed."

"Good work, Sherlock," smiled Pedro. "That's how it works . . . most of the time."

"So it changes sometimes?"

"You've got to get this through your head: nothing is carved in stone at LATCH. It's like the moon, ever-changing. But, for the moment, you can expect this basic format."

"Do we meet every night?" asked Wendy, her desperation to know apparent in her tone.

"The way to live with LATCH is to follow your normal routine and go to bed each night expecting nothing. Sometimes the moon is visible and sometimes it's covered with clouds. But it's always up there, waiting."

"So we have LATCH when the moon is out?" Wendy eagerly deduced.

Pedro looked exasperated. "That was just a comparison, Wendy. You couldn't see the moon last night, could you?"

"No."

Pedro finished, "You don't have to do anything except wear your moon key when you go to bed every night. . . ."

"Which I always wear," Wendy interrupted.

"Right. You don't have to wear special shoes or clothes. Those details will be taken care of. . . ."

Wendy couldn't help interrupting again. "But Phillip wore his bathing suit for the sea lions. Helena must tell him everything. Why can't you tell me?"

Pedro's face tightened. "Helena doesn't tell Phillip. She understands that the revelations are supposed to be experienced with no preparation. Who was better off ultimately . . . you or Phillip with his bathing suit?"

Wendy remembered how her clothes had not gotten in the way or even gotten wet. "Me, I guess."

"Right. You've got to trust me. And steer clear of Phillip," Pedro added.

Wendy could tell by Pedro's expression that he'd heard about last night. "He hates me, doesn't he?"

"Look, Petavius came to me himself and asked me to be your buddy. I think that Phillip heard about Pet's interest in you and is jealous. Obviously, Phillip wants to be the best."

Wendy's heart sank. "I thought Phillip hated me because I'm not from a well-known family and don't have lots of money. But it's because of Petavius?"

"I'm not really sure. The only way to know is to ask Pet."

Wendy was too awed by Petavius to ask him anything.

"But don't worry about Phillip. My best advice is to hang loose and enjoy every moment of the revelations," Pedro said encouragingly.

Wendy thought that it would be stupid to let Phillip ruin the most amazing thing that had ever happened to her. "I'm learning that hanging loose is not one of my strong points. But I'll try. I promise."

"So, LATCH is working already." Pedro smiled. "Oh, by the way, if this is any help, I seem to remember that the three revelations are several nights apart to give everyone a chance to think about how they reacted.

"And, another thing . . . ," Pedro continued. "It might be a good idea to keep a journal. Your memory of the night begins to fade as soon as you wake up. Writing it down keeps the details fresh."

Wendy's face lit up. She was so happy to have a suggestion of something she could actively do, instead of just waiting. "Maybe putting everything down in black and white will help me believe that LATCH really happened."

Pedro turned as if to leave. Wendy didn't want him to go. "Are you allowed to tell me what phase you're in?" she blurted out.

Pedro smiled. "Of course. This is my third phase, the Half Moon Phase. LATCH buddies are always Half Mooners. The theory is that we're experienced enough to be helpful, but not too far removed to remember those first-year feelings."

"Does each phase have a name?" Wendy asked.

Pedro nodded. "True to the phases of the moon,

LATCH phases progress from New Moon to Crescent Moon to Half Moon to Gibbous Moon to Full Moon. As you know, the moon gets bigger in each phase, just like your knowledge and skills at LATCH. Of course, in the case of the moon, it starts to shrink back or wane after it's full until it disappears again."

Wendy was dying to ask Pedro a thousand more questions, but Pedro was heading back down the fire escape. *"Buenos nochas,"* he called.

"Buenos nochas," replied Wendy, and then he was gone.

Wendy stood on the roof for a while just staring at the sky and thinking about all the things Pedro had told her. Then she spotted the tiniest sliver of a crescent moon on the horizon. Without realizing it, a smile appeared on her face, mirroring the moon's curve.

Chapter Eleven

Wendy had written in her new journal for three days. She was running out of material, though, because there had been no more LATCH sessions. Pedro had said it might be a few days between revelations, but it was getting harder and harder to be patient. She thought about calling April, but, she didn't want to seem overeager.

She was just looking under her bed, checking that her notebook was safely hidden for the night, when a soft meow caught her attention. She looked up to find a small gray and black cat peering at her through the window.

Wendy heard a lot of cats out in the alley at night. But she had never seen a cat on the fire escape right outside her window before. Politely, the cat waited on the other side of the glass, staring at Wendy with luminous green eyes.

Something seemed so familiar about this cat. Without thinking, Wendy opened her window. Delicately, the cat stepped in. She was purring. Wendy couldn't resist petting her soft fur. That's when she noticed the cat's collar. It had a moon crescent hanging from it. Fascinated, Wendy touched the tiny silver moon. Unlike her necklace, it was a hinged locket. With trembling fingers, Wendy slid her fingernail into the opening. In it was a tiny folded piece of paper, very much like a fortune in a fortune cookie. Carefully, she unfolded it.

Wendy,
  This is Shadow, my friend. I'll meet you by the row boat rental in Central Park tomorrow at 2:00 P.M.
    —April

Wendy scooped up the cat and kissed her. "Thank you so much, Shadow," she whispered. She wanted to give the cat a treat, but before she could find one, Shadow gracefully leapt out over the windowsill and down the fire escape. It was only then that Wendy began to wonder how Shadow had known where to find her.

She quickly dismissed her logical thought. Who cared? The moon ruled her world now. And anything could happen under the influence of the moon. She clutched the tiny slip of paper in her hand and couldn't wait for tomorrow. She closed her eyes, willing herself to go to sleep.

Bong, bong, bong, bong . . .

Wendy looked up. She was at the bottom of an enormous three-sided set of stone steps. And then someone grabbed her hand and started pulling her up the steps. It was April.

"I guess we'll have a lot to talk about tomorrow."
April grinned.

Wendy was bursting with excitement. It must be
their second revelation. "Do you know where we
are?"

"We're at the Metropolitan Museum of Art, you
idiot," an impatient voice said through the darkness.
"It's a world-famous museum housing a huge selec-
tion of artistic treasures. My family has a whole wing
named after them," Phillip added self-importantly.

"Bully for you," April replied. "My family has a dry
cleaners named after them."

Wendy and April burst out laughing. Phillip looked
like he wanted to slap them both. However, he con-
trolled himself and disappeared through the revolv-
ing door.

April pushed on the door, expecting it to open
like it had for Phillip. It didn't budge. "How did he
get in?"

Wendy thought for a moment. "Could it have
something to do with our moon keys? Pedro told me
to always wear it."

"Good thinking," April said. She pulled out her
necklace and instantly a tiny moon reflection
sparkled on the glass door. April lined up the tiny
light over the keyhole and the door moved without
resistance.

Wendy and April entered the enormous vaulted
lobby of the museum. It was completely empty except for the eight kids from their group.

"Good evening, Humorum Group," a dulcet voice
echoed through the hall.

Wendy and April looked around to find the source
of the voice. And then, from behind a group of lilies

in one of the giant flower arrangements to the left of the main staircase, a face appeared.

"It's that woman from the first night," April whispered.

"I call her Titania," said Wendy, thinking of *A Midsummer Night's Dream*.

The woman slipped out from behind the huge urn. She was dressed in a robe, that glimmered with the palest pastel colors and made her look like a Grecian goddess. She had a streak of orange lily pollen on her cheek. "We meet again," she said, smiling. "You may recognize me from the first night of LATCH. I am Diana. I work with Petavius.

"This is your second revelation. It's my favorite because it's very simple and lots of fun. Just go up the staircase and pick out your favorite painting. Then, project your moon key on the painting and enjoy the rest. I will be around to help anyone who needs it, but I assure you, there will be no polar bears tonight."

April and Wendy joined the rest of the group as they ran up the stairs. Right at the top of the steps was a room with an enormous painting that seemed to be at least twenty feet high. It was a historical painting called *The Triumph of Marius*. The central figure, obviously Marius, was a Roman general dressed in white, standing in his chariot pulled by three snorting steeds. He was looking down at a man in red robes.

Wendy winced when she saw the painting. "I hate this one. Marius looks like such a nasty man. Let's move on," she urged April.

"Please don't," came a voice. "This is my favorite." It was then that they noticed Phillip standing in the shadows.

"I was waiting for you," he added with a smile that looked more like a sneer.

Wendy had a bad feeling. "Why?" she asked.

Phillip didn't answer. Instead he pulled out his moon key, flashed it at Wendy and then aimed it at the man in red robes. Wendy felt a whirling sensation and then her world went black.

When she opened her eyes again it took Wendy a few seconds to figure out where she was, who she was. Every muscle in her body ached as if she'd been beaten. Suddenly, she understood that she was now in the painting in the body of the man in the red robes, the African king, Jukharta, who had just been captured by Marius.

Three horses were snorting and pawing behind her. But Wendy did not flinch. Slowly, she turned around and there was Marius, the hateful Roman general who had conquered her country. Deliberately, she gathered the last bit of saliva in her mouth and spit at him.

Enraged, Marius leapt out of the chariot and charged at her. Wendy watched his face come closer. She was not surprised at who she saw. It was Phillip. He had become Marius. They were in the painting now. It was alive.

Phillip reached for her throat. Wendy was sure he was going to choke her. But instead he tore off her moon necklace.

"No," she cried frantically. It was her most prized possession. She lunged to get it back, but with the iron chains on her arms she was too slow. Phillip triumphantly dropped it into his robe.

"Shall we kill him, sir?" asked one of the soldiers.

Phillip stared at Wendy. "No, bring him to my tent. I have other plans for him."

Some time later, Wendy woke up to the soft whinnying of a horse. She must have passed out from pain and dehydration. She was on the floor of a gold and red silk tent. It was stifling hot. All she could think of was water.

Phillip strode in followed by several servants. "Something is wrong with one of my horses," he declared. "Settle her down."

The servants set down a basin of water and disappeared. Wendy couldn't believe it. The answer to her prayers. She lunged for the water, but Phillip plunged his filthy brown feet into it first. He watched her face collapse and roared with laughter.

Then Phillip jerked his head up. There was a disturbance outside. His horse was out of control. From the inside of the tent, they could see the horse's giant shadow bucking and kicking the rippling silk wall.

This was her moment. Wendy threw the water in Phillip's face just as the wild white horse came pounding into the tent. The horse reared up on its back legs over Phillip. Phillip covered his head and screamed as the enormous beast's hooves descended upon him. In that split second, Wendy reached into his robe pocket and grabbed her necklace.

Instantly, the horse changed tactics. Without touching Phillip, it spun around and moved to Wendy. Wendy reacted instinctively and leaped onto its back. The horse galloped out of the tent.

Only when they were far enough away to be safe from Marius's men did the animal slow its pace and stop. Wendy slid off the horse and came eye to eye with the beast. That was when Wendy knew.

Trembling, she flashed her moon key on the horse and then herself.

* * *

Panting, Wendy and April arrived back in the museum. "Thank you," Wendy whispered shakily.

"I couldn't leave you in there alone with him," April breathed.

"How in the world did you decide to become the horse?" asked Wendy.

"I just knew it was going to take brute force. The horse was the strongest one in there," April explained. "I'm afraid that's the only thing that Phillip understands. The Huntingtons are a family that is all about power."

They silently took stock of themselves. Except for being scared to death, they were unhurt. Neither of them were bruised or bore any physical signs of the adventure they'd survived.

"It seemed so real in there. If Phillip had killed me, would I really have died?" asked Wendy unsteadily.

"I don't think so," said April. "But you might have been trapped in the painting forever."

"Thank goodness, you're all right." Phillip's loud voice made both girls jump as he strode into the room with Diana right behind him. "I've explained to Diana what happened. How you accidentally got beamed into my painting . . . how the character of Marius took over . . . I never imagined he would be so cruel. I always loved that painting as a child. But, the reality of it was horrible."

Phillip approached Wendy, a concerned expression on his face. "I am so sorry." He sounded sincere.

Wendy was at a loss for words. How could Phillip lie so convincingly? Did Diana believe his story? Wendy couldn't tell from the woman's neutral expression. But her eyes watched the three of them closely and Wendy thought maybe, just maybe, Diana wasn't buying his story completely either.

"We'll talk later," Diana said gently. "You two better go and find your own paintings. I'd suggest something a little less dramatic."

"I don't think he knew I was the horse," whispered April as they walked off.

"I'll never tell," Wendy promised.

Chapter Twelve

Wendy and April wandered far away from the European paintings and Phillip. Soon they were in a different exhibit: the Impressionists.

"Imagine a painting coming to life. I will never forgive Phillip for ruining this for us," April fumed.

"If we let him ruin this experience, he'll have won," Wendy said.

"You're right," April agreed. "Hey, look at this one." April stopped in front of a painting of a sailboat by Monet called *The Green Wave*.

Just the sight of the swelling ocean made Wendy feel sick. "You know me and water. That's the last painting I'd pick. But you go ahead. I'll stay out here, and if you're not out in a half hour, I'll come in and get you."

April appeared touched. "You'd brave the water for me, even though it terrifies you?"

"I want to make sure that Phillip doesn't try to hurt you," Wendy said firmly.

"I don't think he will tonight. Anyhow, he's out for your hide, not mine."

"Not when he finds out that your hide was the horse's," Wendy teased.

April was just about to enter the painting when she spotted another. She stared at the two rosy-cheeked girls in the French countryside for a minute, then moved to study the painting more closely.

"They look like us, one dark and one blonde. Sort of like sisters. It's called *In the Meadow* by Renoir." April read from the plaque on the wall. "I've changed my mind. I'd like to go into this one, but only if you'll come with me."

Wendy looked around the hall. No Phillip. "Looks good to me. I don't see any water."

They took out their moon keys. "One, two, three," they said in unison.

Suddenly, they were in the meadow. For two city girls, it was an awakening. The warm sun danced on their faces. April wiggled her bare toes in the soft grass. "Oh, this is the best."

Wendy stared at April. "I don't think we're talking in English, but I understand you."

"We're probably speaking French, since we're in France. C'mon, let's explore." April jumped up and ran off. "I think I see a stream."

"Look, someone's having a picnic," said Wendy. Nestled in the curve of the stream was a red-checkered tablecloth and a basket.

Immediately, April sat down and started unpacking the basket.

"Wait a minute," Wendy said. "We don't know that this is our picnic."

April stopped. "It has to be. I just know it is."

Wendy wasn't convinced until she spied two pairs of shoes and stockings under a tree. She tried on the bigger pair of shoes. They fit perfectly. She held up the other pair to April. "If these fit you, we eat."

April slipped them on like Cinderella. "I told you," she said impatiently as she dove into the goodies.

Even though they didn't recognize half of what they ate, Wendy and April had never had a more delicious meal. The bread and butter alone were the best they'd ever had.

When they were finished Wendy patted her stomach. "I'm stuffed. Let's go wading."

"You want to go into the water? That's a first," April teased.

"I think I can manage this shallow stream," Wendy responded.

The water was cool, but not cold, swirling around their ankles. The smooth pebbles massaged the soles of their feet. Before long, they were dancing, twirling, splashing and shrieking. April tagged Wendy. "You're it!"

Wendy chased April, lunged to tag her and lost her balance. Wendy's swipe knocked April over. Laughing, they both ended up sitting in the water. April noticed two pebbles in the stream. One was white and the other was rose colored. "One for each of us." She handed Wendy the pale one. "Our sister stones," she murmured solemnly, "so we can remember this day . . . always."

Wendy held the tiny pebble. Despite the cool stream, it seemed almost warm. She would treasure it.

"I wonder what it would be like if we never went back," whispered April.

Wendy thought about this. "You know, this is a

wonderful place. But I'd miss the boys, I'd miss being Wendy Hilton. I'm not sure I'd want to be a French girl in a long white dress forever."

April nodded reluctantly. "I guess I'd miss my parents, but I wouldn't miss working at the dry cleaners. However, I suppose I couldn't be elected the President of the United States if I was here."

"You want to be president?" Wendy asked.

"Why not," April retorted. "I like being the boss."

Wendy laughed. "That's true."

They stood up and wrung out their skirts. Then they reached for their necklaces; that's when April's face went pink, like her dress. "My moon key's gone."

"Don't panic. I can always get you back," Wendy reassured her.

"But it was my grandmother's. I don't know if I can stay in LATCH without it," April worried.

Wendy looked around them. "It's got to be here somewhere."

Inch by inch, they searched the brown and gray pebbles, but they couldn't find it. Wendy was worried about getting back before the LATCH session ended. She wondered if Diana would be able to find them if they didn't come back in time.

A ray of orange sunlight broke through the foliage, spotlighting the water. That's when Wendy spotted a flash of silver. Just as Wendy reached in, it disappeared into the mouth of a small speckled fish. "Oh no you don't," she cried as she grabbed the fish. The two girls scrambled out of the water and Wendy placed the fish on the tablecloth where it flipped around frantically.

"He didn't swallow the whole thing yet," Wendy noticed with excitement. Ever so gently, she tugged the chain and then the moon out of the fish's mouth.

Triumphantly, she handed the necklace to April and put the fish back in the stream, unharmed.

"I owe you," April said gratefully.

"After saving me in Phillip's painting, not to mention the sea lions?" Wendy scoffed. "I don't think so."

"Let's go," April said. "Enough country life for me."

They were back in their original clothes, dry as a bone, standing in front of the painting. "I don't think we have much time for your painting." April was concerned.

"Don't be silly. That one can count for mine, too. It was heaven," Wendy assured her.

"But, it wasn't your choice. It doesn't seem fair to me," April said. They were making their way back to the lobby when Wendy spotted it. She froze.

April continued walking, unaware that Wendy was not by her side anymore. Entranced by the world before her, Wendy reached for her moon key almost unconsciously.

This time, Wendy felt entirely different. This time, she wasn't a lumbering man or a teenager in a French meadow. This time, her legs were rubbery and barely held her up. This time, she looked up at the world from a vantage point of about two feet. She was only a year old.

She didn't notice the vegetable garden or the ivy-covered cottage or the wheelbarrow full of hay. The only thing she was aware of was the feel and smell of her mother as she held Wendy and the sight of her smiling father holding out his arms to catch her. Wendy's heart beat excitedly. It was time. The three of them knew that this was the moment.

Lovingly, Wendy's mother set her on the ground.

Wendy took a deep breath, puffed out her lips with concentration and threw up her arms to propel herself. Fiercely, she willed her chubby legs to move. Wendy's eyes widened as they did just that. She couldn't believe it. Step by tottering step, she was actually walking. She didn't fall down as she had countless times before. Row by row, she passed the vegetables that her father had been hoeing.

In a flash, in an eternity, Wendy reached her father's warm, calloused hands. He scooped her up, laughing and rejoicing. *Bravo!* She had done it! She had taken her first steps.

And then her mother was by their side, hugging both of them, cheering, kissing Wendy's temple. A perfectly balanced circle of love. Somewhere deep inside of her, Wendy remembered this feeling. Wendy willed this moment to never end.

And then, she felt the whisper of a hand on her shoulder. She pulled away. *No!* There was the hint of Diana's voice, "I'm sorry, Wendy. Time to go."

Wendy felt herself slipping away from the painting. "I know this is hard for you," Diana murmured.

Wendy resisted. "I don't want to go back . . ."

But before she could finish, the struggle was over and Wendy was standing in the cold, artificial light of the museum, squeezing her eyes shut, trying to hold onto that golden moment with adoring parents. Her face was wet.

April stood silently as Wendy and Diana reappeared. They were in front of Van Gogh's *First Steps*. April smiled sympathetically at Wendy. A mother in a blue dress, a father in work clothes and a tiny girl in a white bonnet, about to walk for the first time, presented a compelling picture.

Wendy's vision was blurry. She felt dizzy and sick

and happy. Happier than she could ever remember feeling.

"Your parents loved you that way, too," Diana said softly.

"They did?" Wendy asked tremulously.

"I'm sure they did," Diana assured her. "It's midnight."

"See you tomorr—"

Before April could finish, Wendy heard the now familiar rushing sound.

Wendy lay motionless in her bed, her heart racing. If she concentrated, she could just manage to hear the bees and feel the sun as the warmth of her parents' love surrounded her. She willed herself to fall asleep with those images filling her head.

Chapter Thirteen

Wendy was very groggy when she woke up the next day, as if her mind refused to let go of her dreams. They had been so rich, so complicated. She couldn't wait to discuss them with April.

She was half afraid that April wouldn't show up, but she was waiting by the boathouse as planned. "How did you talk your parents into letting you come?" asked Wendy.

April smiled proudly. "I talked my older cousin into bringing me. They trust him. He's out on the lake rowing with his girlfriend."

They followed a path around the lake and climbed to an enormous rock outcrop perched over the water. "So what did you think of our second revelation?" Wendy asked.

"I loved being a horse," April confessed. "I woke up with the sensation of being that powerful mare."

"You probably loved being so big, because you're so tiny," Wendy teased.

April thought about that. "Maybe that was part of

it," she agreed. "But I also liked being transformed into a completely different creature."

"Weren't you frustrated that you couldn't speak?" asked Wendy.

"Not at all," April replied. "Maybe, because part of me was still April and could think in words. I wish I knew whether animals think or not." April grinned mischievously. "And I loved scaring Phillip to death." They both laughed.

April tilted her head to the side. "Actually, my favorite LATCH moments so far have been swimming with the sea lions and becoming a horse. I've always loved animals."

"I should have guessed that. You were a natural sea lion. You talked to the eagles. By the way, I loved your messenger, Shadow. How did you manage that?"

April shrugged. "Some people use pigeons. Shadow and I are very close." She didn't elaborate, instead switching the subject. "I still can't believe what Phillip did to you. He seems to know how all the revelations work in advance."

"Oh, I meant to tell you," Wendy said growing animated. "Pedro said that Phillip is getting information about the revelations from someone who is ultimately going to hurt his chances of surviving LATCH."

"I wonder who's filling him in?" asked April.

"Pedro said that it wasn't Helena. But Phillip did say that he has a lot of family members who attended LATCH."

"It doesn't sound like they're doing him any favors, though," April said. "That's my biggest fear—getting kicked out. I wonder if a lot of kids get asked to leave. Or more accurately, since we don't actually do anything to go there, do some people just stop getting whisked away in the middle of the night?"

Wendy cringed. "That's a horrible thought. It's bad enough never knowing when we're going to have a revelation. It would be worse though, to wait and wait and never go anywhere. I would die. LATCH has been the best thing that's ever happened to me."

"I'm not surprised, since you met me there," teased April. "We've just got to take it a day at a time, accept the wonder of it and not worry about what's going to happen tomorrow. Even if it ends, it has already been worth it."

"Would you stop being so sensible?" Wendy groaned in frustration.

"I can't help it. Maybe, that's why I like animals so much. They accept their world as it is."

"Well, I'm not so accepting," Wendy said. "My life would be a lot easier without Phillip Huntington the Fourth."

"Are you going to tell Diana or Petavius that he purposely sent you into the painting?" April asked quietly.

"I don't want to. . . ." Wendy struggled to explain her feelings. "I'd hate to get anyone kicked out of LATCH."

"But that's exactly what he's trying to do to you! Trying to get you kicked out . . . or killed!" April's charcoal eyes flashed fire.

"If he succeeds, I'll have to say something. But, somehow I feel like I'm meant to survive, despite Phillip. It's sort of like he's part of the process."

"I hope you're not being foolish." April sighed.

"I hope not, too," Wendy agreed. "But, you know what you said about appreciating the good things we've already gotten from LATCH, even if it ended today." Wendy reached into her pocket and pulled out her white pebble. "Well, you're right. I always wanted a sister. And now, I feel like I have one."

April reached into her pocket to show Wendy that she had her rose pebble with her. "Me too."

They hugged. Wendy laughed, "Some dream."

April smiled in anticipation. "Can you imagine what the third revelation will be like?"

Chapter Fourteen

A few days went by and Wendy began to get restless again. She checked her calendar to pinpoint the arrival of the next full moon, which was on Friday. She hoped that it might coincide with the third revelation.

Unfortunately, the weather in Manhattan was very unpleasant. Each day got muggier, heavier and more oppressive than the day before. By Friday, the tension was so thick that the whole world felt like it might explode. Wendy had just tucked the boys into bed when the first booming thunderclap made her jump. She stared at the flashing sky thinking that this was no night to hold LATCH. The rain slammed against her window. She settled down, resigned to spend an uneventful night.

There was another burst of lightning and a boom of thunder and Wendy had the feeling that she was flying on a cloud of light and sound. And then she was in a small, dark, round room. A double staircase took up a large part of the space. It didn't seem possible, but her whole LATCH group, plus Petavius, was squished into the remaining space. Before Wendy could say anything, a deafening percussion of thunder, louder than Wendy had ever heard before, filled the room. It was as if they were inside an enormous metal drum. The walls seemed to reverberate.

Finally, the rumbling subsided and Petavius could be heard. "Good evening. Well, well, well. I can't remember the last time our third revelation was held on such a dramatic evening. Some powerful magic is here tonight."

Another cannon shot of thunder almost knocked them over. Wendy could feel the floor sway. April squeezed Wendy's hand. "Have any of you guessed where you are yet?" Pet asked.

Phillip jumped up to answer. Pet cut him off abruptly, "Not you. I asked if any of you had guessed, not been told." Phillip sat back down, muttering, "I don't know what the big deal is about being prepared."

Another display of lightning illuminated the walls. Wendy saw giant curved lines. "It looks like hair on a giant head," she blurted out impulsively.

April peered out one of the small windows. "I see water and the Manhattan skyline."

Petavius smiled. "You're both correct. We are inside the crown of the Statue of Liberty. This part is no longer open to the public."

A gasp went up among the group. Many of them had been to the statue for class trips. But they would never have guessed where they were.

"We visit Libertas, the Goddess of Liberty, for our third revelation because of what she stands for: freedom, opportunity and the courage to stand for what you believe in. Traits we look for in each LATCH participant."

Pet continued, "We traditionally hold the third revelation on the night of the full moon. Despite the storm clouds, I can assure you that the moon's full power is shining down on all of you. It should help you in the challenge ahead. Tonight is really very simple. Just one exercise. However, you will participate one at a time.

"Miss Hilton . . ." Wendy jumped as Petavius called her name. Oh no. She dreaded going first. "I'd like you to go last."

Last. What did that mean? Wendy sensed the others were wondering the same thing, and she felt terribly self-conscious. Phillip glared at her.

An earsplitting explosion shook the room. Even Pet seemed a little breathless when he spoke, "Don't worry. This statue was designed by Alexandre Gustave Eiffel, the talented sculptor and engineer also responsible for the Eiffel Tower in Paris. This lady's copper skin can actually move independently of her skeletal framework and the total structure is designed to sway a few inches in high winds. It has a safety system to absorb lightning and ground it. We're perfectly safe.

"So, Tamara Johnson, would you like to come with me?" Wendy gulped as a tall, dark-haired girl moved down the steps with Pet. "The rest of you stay up here until it's your turn," Pet added as he disappeared.

The remaining kids formed a ring on the floor, except for Phillip, who walked over to the window. Everyone stared at each other awkwardly until April broke the ice by introducing herself. Then everyone started talking at once until Tamara reappeared with a big smile on her face. She escorted the next boy down, but didn't come back.

One by one, they disappeared. Soon, it was just

Phillip, Wendy, and April. Phillip still stood by the window, studiously ignoring the two girls. His pompous attitude made Wendy want to roll her eyes. He was so ridiculous. She'd never met such a snob.

Unfortunately, she happened to look in April's direction just in time to catch April rolling *her* eyes. That was all it took. A deep, endless tickle of laughter bubbled up from the core of Wendy's being. It was too much—the heat, the anticipation, the storm, the situation. She couldn't stop herself. She started laughing uncontrollably.

In seconds, April had joined her. Phillip moved to stand over the two of them holding their sides in hysterics. "Are you laughing at me?" he demanded. He looked angry enough to hit one of them and took a menacing step closer, his hands balled up in fists.

"Don't even think about it," snapped a voice. The last boy, Nick, materialized from the shadow of the stairs. Phillip spun around.

"Why am I not surprised that you're the type to hit girls? Big man," Nick sneered. "What a tough guy. Don't try any of that stuff when I'm around. It would be a real pleasure to pop you one. April is next."

"I'm not going without Wendy," April said, wiping the tears of laughter from her face.

Wendy stared at Phillip until he met her gaze. "No, you go ahead. This is the way Pet wants it. We'll be fine, won't we, Phillip?"

Phillip nodded. Reluctantly, April and Nick moved down the stairs.

For awhile, Wendy and Phillip said nothing. Finally, Phillip spoke. "The storm seems to have passed."

"I've seen some lightning, but no thunder," Wendy observed.

Phillip's mouth curved with what Wendy could

have sworn was a smirk. "I don't think that's lightning." Then his tone turned accusatory. "You told him, didn't you?"

"What are you talking about?"

"You told Petavius that I beamed you into the painting and that's why he cut me off tonight."

A power that Wendy had no idea she possessed welled up inside of her. She spoke as if to a wild animal, low and firm. "You listen to me. I have not told Petavius a thing. Which is *not* a promise that I won't in the future. He cut you off because you're not supposed to know about the revelations. Pedro told me that whoever is telling you is getting you into trouble. Helena is upset. She's afraid you're going to get kicked out of LATCH!"

Phillip went nuts. "I should have known, you tattletale. You talked to Pedro and he talked to Petavius!"

Wendy flared, "I talked to Pedro after our first revelation at the zoo. He doesn't have any idea how you tortured me in that painting. So he couldn't possibly have talked to Pet. The main thing he told me was to ignore you. Which I would dearly love to do. What have I ever done to you to make you hate me so much?"

A paint box of emotions spattered over Phillip's face. "I know why Petavius wants you to go last. I've sensed it from the beginning." For a second, Wendy thought she was going to hear the whole story. Then, he threw her a curveball. "Where did you get your moon key?"

Reflexively, Wendy's hand flew to her neck. Phillip, as Marius, had ripped her moon key off in the painting. She was afraid he might do it again. "Why do you care?" she challenged him.

At that moment, April raced back into the room. She looked worried as she glanced between the two of them.

"I'm fine," Wendy assured her.

April grabbed Phillip's arm. "Your turn," she said as she propelled him out of the room.

Wendy knew that it wasn't over with Phillip. But he was gone for now. The room seemed abnormally still. Even the lightning seemed to have disappeared.

She realized she was trembling and closed her eyes; she had to calm down before it was her turn. She took a couple of deep breaths and tried to imagine a soothing image. Suddenly, she felt the love and peace she'd experience when she was the baby learning to walk in the painting. Her breathing slowed. Her hands stopped shaking. Time stopped.

"Your turn . . ." Phillip was back already. That was quick.

Silently, Phillip led the way down the narrow metal staircase to an open trap door which gave way to a metal tunnel with a ladder inside of it. "You climb up there."

It was a little creepy. Wendy made her way up the long, vertical tube. The only light came from an opening at the top. Pet's face appeared in the opening. He reached down to pull her up. Suddenly, Wendy was outdoors on a narrow catwalk overlooking the New York harbor.

Pet smiled. "This is somewhere very special. No visitors have been allowed up here for eighty years. You are standing on the torch of the Statue of Liberty, three hundred and five feet above the ground."

Wendy stared at the golden flames in disbelief. She realized that she had climbed up the whole right arm of Libertas and was perched high in the sky.

"Do you feel dizzy?" asked Petavius with concern.

Surprisingly, Wendy felt exhilarated. "No. It's fantastic. The top of the world. Thank you so much for giving me this experience."

Petavius nodded. "You're welcome." He smiled slightly. "No one else thanked me for the view. Below us, we can see the seven rays of the Statue's crown, which represent the seven seas and continents of the world."

Wendy looked down. This time, her stomach did flip a little. They were up so high. The rain had stopped, but there were no stars, no moon visible.

Petavius stared at Wendy. "As you know, LATCH is the Lunar Arena of Transformation, Concentration and *Hope*. These are our three guiding concepts. What I'd like you to do now is to close your eyes and concentrate on the light of the torch. That light signifies hope to many people. As you think about the torch, I'd like you to think about hope, about what it represents, and the power it has to make dreams come true."

Wendy closed her eyes. At first her thoughts were fuzzy. It was hard to think about hope, in general. But then, she thought about the hope she'd had the night of her birthday when she'd vowed to make a life for herself. She thought about the incredible hope she had felt after her first night at LATCH. Finally, she let the deeply buried hope that someday she would find out what had happened to her parents bubble up inside her. The image of the golden torch blazed in her mind. It was so powerful that Wendy even felt her eyelids fill with a radiant aura of light.

"Very good," Pet murmured. "You can stop."

Wendy opened her eyes and realized that the

clouds had suddenly parted and now, the full moon, in all its glory, was beaming down upon them.

"Oh, that's why it got so bright," Wendy said.

Pet gave her one of his secret smiles. "That's one of the reasons." Wendy sensed that he wanted to tell her something more, but then the moon slipped behind a cloud and he seemed to change his mind. "You can go now. And I almost forgot, Phillip is coming back to talk to me."

Wendy was surprised. Pet had said that she would be the last one. A little confused, she started down the ladder. She gasped when her foot touched the bottom rung and someone grabbed it.

"Don't scream," hissed Phillip.

Now what did he want?

"I knew it," he muttered jealously. "You lit up the whole sky."

Wendy didn't know what he was ranting about.

Phillip searched her face. Disbelievingly, he asked, "Don't you know why Pet wanted you to go last? He didn't want you to upstage everyone else. Your illumination lasted forever."

Finally, Wendy was beginning to understand what Phillip was talking about. "I was lucky. The full moon came out while I had my eyes closed. It made the sky brighter."

Phillip looked surprised. "You closed your eyes?"

"Pet suggested that," Wendy responded. "It's easier to concentrate."

"You fool! The purpose of the third revelation is finding out how much power each of us has stored inside of us and how well we can focus it. Some kids were able to make the torch flash. Some just made it flicker. But you filled the sky for miles and miles before the moon ever showed its face." He spoke to her as if she were dim-witted. "When we were down in the crown room together, you mentioned that you saw lightning but heard no thunder. Those flashes of light were from the other kids taking their turns. Now do you get it?"

Wendy stared at Phillip. He had told her so many lies. But for some reason, she believed him tonight. Pet had looked pleased.

Phillip grabbed her wrist. "The thing is, you're my only chance." Wendy was astonished as Phillip's face crumpled. "I couldn't do it. I couldn't even make the light flutter," Phillip confessed. "Petavius said he'd give me another chance. But I know I'm already on shaky ground. You've got to understand, LATCH is the most important thing in the world to me and my family. My father was in LATCH. He was brilliant, but he got hurt and never got to finish. All of his hopes and dreams have been invested in me. If I get kicked out, it will kill him. You've got to help me."

Wendy felt as if her whole world had flipped upside down. Snotty, arrogant Phillip was begging her to help him. Maybe that's why he was so impossible. Because underneath it all, he was really scared to death. Despite her better judgment, Wendy's heart reached out to him. "I think what worked for me was focusing on some specific situations where I felt hope. It sounds like if you think about your father you should be fine. . . ."

Phillip cut her off impatiently. "I tried that. It didn't work. I'm no good with hope." Wendy was shocked. Hope was how she got through every day. Hope was how she had survived all those foster families.

Phillip continued fiercely. "This is what I need. After I start up the ladder, I want you to wait two minutes, then concentrate on the torch the way you did before. I'm sure that you're powerful enough to light it from the bottom of the ladder. That should coincide with my second try."

"But that's cheating."

"It's helping," Phillip corrected her adamantly.

"Pet will find out," Wendy protested.

"I have to take the risk. You're my only chance."

Why was Phillip making her feel so guilty? "I really think it's all inside of you, Phillip," Wendy repeated. "Just think about your father. . . ."

"Phillip?" Pet called.

"Coming," Phillip said. "Two minutes," he whispered. And with that he scrambled up the ladder.

Wendy stood there, shaken. He couldn't make her cheat! Firmly, she turned away and hurried back to the crown room, her mind churning. She couldn't get Phillip's stricken look out of her mind.

From the crown room, the sky was dark. Not a flash of light. She willed Phillip to dig down deep and find the hope that must exist in his heart.

The sky lit up for a split second. Wendy's heart raced. He had done it! She hadn't cheated. Not for one second had she used her own hope to light the torch.

A few minutes later, Wendy heard his footsteps on the stairs. "It worked all the way from here?" he asked incredulously.

"Congratulations," Wendy greeted him firmly. "You did it with no help from me."

"Right," Phillip responded sarcastically. "You do realize that our destinies are intertwined now."

"But I didn't do anything except wish that you would find your own hope," Wendy protested.

Phillip smiled as though he knew better. "I'll be

fine now. Once you make it past the revelations, you're in."

Wendy hated the look in his eyes. She repeated to herself that it couldn't have been her that had enabled Phillip to succeed. He had done it himself. He must have . . .

Wendy didn't hear a clock chime, but suddenly, Phillip was gone. The Statue of Liberty was gone. She was back in her bed.

Chapter Fifteen

Our destinies are intertwined now. . . . Wendy woke up with a jolt at the sound of Phillip's voice. She had been having a nightmare.

Wendy went through the details of the previous night and had a sense of uneasiness. She couldn't help worrying that she had done something wrong. She had tried so hard not to help Phillip cheat. She had ignored his directions. The only thing she had done was wish him the power to find his own hope. But Phillip thought she'd helped him. He seemed so sure. It made her doubt herself.

A light pressure landed on her bed, and she flipped around. Two unblinking green eyes took her measure. Wendy scooped up Shadow. Eagerly, Wendy reached for Shadow's locket.

> *Working all day. Stop by the dry cleaners if possible.*
> *—A*

Wendy hugged Shadow gratefully. That's just what she needed. She would sort out this mess with April.

The bell jangled as Wendy pushed open the glass door of Lucky Moon Dry Cleaners. April was barely visible from behind a rack of clothing bags.

"You made it! I can take a quick break. Let's go to the park.

"I've been so worried about you. Did Phillip behave himself or did he try something?" April said, cutting right to the chase as they walked outside.

Wendy hesitated. Now that she was here, she realized she wasn't sure what she wanted to tell April. "We talked. I did see another side of him. He's got a lot of pressure on him because of his father."

April looked skeptical. "I hope you're not going soft on him. He's a snake."

"He accused me of ratting on him to Petavius about the painting. But I set him straight." Wendy decided that April deserved to know this.

"He must have loved that." April grinned as they found an empty park bench and sat down. "So, how long did you get the torch to burn?"

"Actually, I closed my eyes. I'm not sure," Wendy responded. "But forget about me, how did you do?"

"The torch flamed for three seconds." April couldn't keep the pride from her voice.

"That's great," Wendy said warmly.

April appeared pleased. "Pet seemed happy. Why did you go last, do you know?"

Wendy wasn't sure what to say. She only had Phillip's word for it. How could she tell April that he had said it was because she was the most powerful? It sounded like bragging. "No, I don't."

April grew animated. "I was thinking about it all morning. Did you notice how the flashes in the sky grew longer and longer as Petavius went through the group? Of course, I didn't see you and Phillip go, but I think Petavius wanted you to be last because he knew that you would be the best." April didn't sound jealous. "How did Phillip do?"

Wendy couldn't figure out how to tell April about Phillip's disaster. "I wasn't really paying attention. But, when I was alone, waiting for Phillip, I didn't notice the sky lighting up at all."

April loved this idea. "Wouldn't that be great if Phillip fell flat on his face after being so obnoxious? Serves him right."

April's glee made Wendy uncomfortable. She realized that she couldn't tell April what had happened after all. "I think that Phillip is a force to be reckoned with, even if he didn't light up the torch."

April nodded. "I agree. It's just that this exercise was about hope, a positive emotion. I think Phillip would be better at hate, jealousy, revenge—negative feelings. The question is, will Phillip's strengths help him at LATCH? After all, the moon is about light."

"The moon has a light and a *dark* side," murmured Wendy.

That gave them both pause.

"You're right." April jumped up. "Gotta get back. I wonder what comes after the third revelation. I hope we don't have to wait too long."

"It's been a few days between each revelation. Don't hold your breath," Wendy warned. "Oh, I almost forgot. Phillip told me that if we make it through the three revelations, we're in."

"I can't stand the suspense," April confessed. "I'm

going to use my powers of concentration and make LATCH come soon, so we'll know for sure."

"Works for me." Wendy laughed.

April rushed off, but Wendy sat there for a long time thinking about lightness . . . and darkness.

Chapter Sixteen

That night Wendy lay in bed wishing that she had told April what had happened with Phillip. Her silence made her feel even guiltier than she had felt before. She stared out the window as a big slice of a huge orange ball appeared over the horizon. It was the moon, nearly full. The opposite of last night, the sky was crystal clear and every little shadow of the moon's surface was visible. Within seconds, the whole moon appeared and rose in the sky, changing from orange to yellow to a brilliant, shimmering white. It seemed almost alive. Wendy couldn't take her eyes off it.

She was unaware that she had fallen asleep. *Bong, bong, bong, bong . . .*

Pedro's eyes and teeth sparkled. They were going somewhere together. They soared up to a very high point. The wind made their hair dance. On a stone terrace, six curved rows of pearly white chairs glowed in the moonlight. A number of people had already arrived. Something important was about to take place.

"Where are we?" Wendy whispered to Pedro.

"We are at a very special place called Belvedere Castle, in the middle of Central Park. This is where the LATCH initiation is always held."

"Initiation? Does that mean that I made it?"

Pedro started laughing. "Of course you made it. There was never any doubt. The rumor is, you may have the most potential of all."

Wendy was a little embarrassed, but thrilled by the compliment. She looked down and realized that she was wearing a soft white dress. "My clothes!"

"I told you that you never had to worry about dressing appropriately for LATCH," Pedro said.

Wendy realized that everyone was dressed in white. She and Pedro walked to the front edge of the terrace. From there they could see a small, irregularly shaped pond. For some reason, Wendy shivered.

"That's called Turtle Pond," Pedro said.

Beyond the pond was an open-air theater where summer productions of Shakespeare were staged. "I can't believe I've never been up here before," Wendy said.

"The castle is tucked away north of 79th Street," Pedro explained. "And since the founders of the park didn't believe in signs, it's not that easy to stumble upon." Pedro turned around. "I think it's time to sit down."

Every chair had a luminescently lettered name written on the back. White on white. Like frosting on a wedding cake. They found their chairs in the second row.

Wendy looked around. April was seated right behind her. Wendy almost knocked her chair over to hug April. "We made it!" April said, then introduced her buddy, Adam.

As they were chatting away, an imperious voice cut through. "Pardon me." Phillip moved past Wendy as if he barely knew her. What kind of an act was he playing now?

April leaned up and whispered to Wendy, "Despite blowing it on the torch, it looks like he weaseled his way in. Wonder how he managed that?"

Wendy felt sick. She wished she had told April the whole story.

"Good evening, Initiates, Buddies and Hallowed Senior Members." Petavius welcomed everyone. Diana stood at his side in a long, flowing gown. "This is a very important evening at the Lunar Arena of Transformation, Concentration and Hope. This is the night that we officially welcome our new members into our LATCH family." Wendy felt her throat tighten. Her family . . .

"As you look around, you will notice that of the original thirty-two candidates who were invited to LATCH, thirty of you remain."

Wendy turned slightly and caught April's eye. So two of them hadn't made it.

"We at LATCH are convinced that each of you has unlimited promise and the commitment to develop that potential to its fullest. Occasionally, one of you will choose to leave LATCH. But that is unusual. Barring some blatant and premeditated violation of the LATCH Code, all thirty of you will be sitting here at Belvedere Castle in five years contemplating your boundless futures.

"On that occasion, you will be accompanied not only be your current buddies, but also by the new buddies that you will take under your wings when you are in your third year. At LATCH you are a part of a seamless tapestry of relationships."

Wendy was very moved. LATCH was everything she had ever wanted. She would never do anything to risk getting kicked out. She sat there terrified that somehow what had happened with Phillip last night, despite her best intentions, would backfire on her.

Pedro must have felt her tension, because he leaned in her direction. "Relax, enjoy," he whispered. "This is the best part. After this, you're really going to have to work." Wendy forced herself to smile. Pedro didn't know what she had done.

"If at any point, you do choose to leave LATCH, all you have to do is make up your mind. Only willing participants can be transported to LATCH. You have the power to control your destiny."

Wendy flinched. Pet's words reminded her too much of Phillip's mention of destiny.

"And now, the highlight of our initiation ceremony. When your name is called, please move through the front portico. At that time, you will have the rare privilege of looking into the Moon Mystifier. I know it can be overwhelming. But please pay attention to every detail."

Petavius and Diana walked down a few steps until they were out of sight. Then, as if someone had hit a switch, a bluish-white light shimmered, creating wave-like reflections on the pillars and ceiling.

"Sara Andrews," Pet called. A girl in the first row got up.

Wendy's heart pounded. The alphabet, again. At least this time, she wouldn't be first or last. She could hear Pet and Diana murmuring softly, in turn. What could the Moon Mystifier be? Her imagination ran wild. She was unaware of initiates getting up and down.

And then, Wendy heard her name. Shakily, she got to her feet and walked through the portico.

In front of the castle was another smaller terrace built right on top of the rock. The view was magnificent; she could see the whole park.

More amazing, though, was the Moon Mystifier. It was a full moon made of glass, at least five feet in diameter, hanging on a stand. The glass was molded like the craters and mountains of the moon. The most startling thing was the unearthly light that came from the swirling mist inside the glass. There were no wires or visible batteries. It had a power of its own and glowed with a mystical sheen, just like the moon.

Pet indicated that she could come to his side. "I'd like you to turn now and look into the Moon Mystifier."

Slowly, Wendy turned. At first she saw nothing but the glass moon. Then, the cloudy stuff inside began to shift. An image swirled and formed. It was a chubby little girl, who looked to be about four years old. She was wearing a party dress. Suddenly, the girl's face lit up into a giant smile.

Pet couldn't help smiling. "Do you know what you are seeing?

"It's me, when I was younger," Wendy whispered.

"It's you the way you are inside. The Moon Mystifier shows us different sides of ourselves. You think of yourself like this, like the young girl you were before all your disappointments."

Wendy nodded. It was hard to talk. She missed that little girl who still believed that her parents were coming back. A little girl full of smiles.

Diana motioned her to the other side of the mysti-fier. "This side shows you how other people see you."

Wendy was horrified. The mist had changed. She wasn't a cute little girl anymore. She was disheveled, wearing a torn T-shirt and shorts. Her dirty blond hair was pulled back into a limp ponytail. She looked withdrawn and miserable. She was not smiling.

Wendy suddenly felt angry and oddly disap-pointed with herself. "I look so unhappy."

"Are you unhappy? How would you like to look?" Diana asked.

"Come back over here," Petavius said.

Terrified now, Wendy asked, "Do I have to?"

"I think you're going to like this one," he said softly.

It took every ounce of courage for Wendy to face the sphere again. This time a young woman formed. Her blond hair glistened. She was absolutely stun-ning and dressed in an ice blue gown. Energy crack-led from every pore as the woman reached her arms out for someone. Best of all, her face radiated such happiness that she made Wendy feel good again.

"Who is that?" Wendy asked. And then she knew. "That's my mother, isn't it?" she whispered.

Pet smiled. "I know you're not going to believe this, but the person in the Moon Mystifier is you, the person you have the power to become."

It was impossible. This woman was like a princess, a goddess. How could that possibly be her?

Pet watched Wendy's skeptical face. "Trust me. It just takes hope and work. Welcome to LATCH."

In a blur, Wendy stumbled back to her seat. If only she could become half of what that final image rep-resented. Whatever it took, she would do it.

"Phillip Huntington the Fourth . . ."

Now it was Phillip's turn. At first his viewings seemed uneventful enough. But then the light from the Moon Mystifier started to flicker on and off. Almost as if it was shorting out. Something seemed to be wrong. Phillip's voice grew louder, harsher. Petavius spoke softly but firmly.

A few moments later, Phillip was striding back to his chair. He was smiling his self-satisfied smile as usual. His face looked flushed though, and as he sat down Wendy thought she heard him whisper to Helena, "That thing is crazy."

No one else caused the light show Phillip had. April's session seemed to take no time at all. She returned with her shoulders back and her face full of pride.

And then it was over. Pet and Diana came back to the front.

"Will all of our Initiates please rise," intoned Petavius.

"Having seen what you can become, do all of you wish to commit to the mission of LATCH, to become the best that you can be to make the world a better place?"

Thirty voices answered as one. "We do."

Diana continued, "Do you recognize that once you are part of the LATCH family that you have a bond to each other, to help and support each other any way you can even after you leave here?"

"We do."

Diana smiled. "Each of you has a silver crescent moon which is your key to LATCH. As a token of the step you have taken today, you will notice that your moon has taken on a new luster. Wear it proudly."

Pet and Diana spoke together. "We now welcome you to the New Moon Phase of LATCH."

Wendy let out a cheer. So did everyone else. April inspected Wendy's necklace. "Look, there's a diamond at the top of the crescent." Wendy checked April's. She had one, too.

"You get a diamond for every phase," Pedro explained. He pulled his moon key out for inspection. Sure enough, it had three tiny diamond stars.

There were refreshments and pictures, but finally Wendy and April had a moment to talk. "Wasn't the Moon Mystifier amazing?" April smiled.

Wendy bit her lip as she thought of how miserable she'd looked in the second scene. "My first two images were so different. . . ."

April was surprised. "Mine were almost identical. But the third one was like my wildest dream come true. As if the Mystifier knew what was in my heart."

"What's in your heart then? Do tell us," Phillip mocked.

April's face hardened. "I'd love to hear what happened to you, Phil baby. What was going on with that crazy light show during your turn?"

Phillip snapped, "What did you see exactly?"

"It looked like the Moon Mystifier was having a seizure. All that sparking and flashing. . . ."

Phillip's face relaxed. "The Mystifier went haywire. Pet spent a long time fixing it."

"Interesting that it only went haywire with you," April commented flatly.

"Pet told me it was probably because I was just too powerful," Phillip confessed to them as he glided off.

April rolled her eyes. "I think the Mystifier went haywire because what Phillip has the power to become is a lot of different things, some of them pretty scary."

Wendy wanted to get off the subject of Phillip. "Let's go try some of those cookies that change shape like the moon. If you time it right, you can get a full moon."

Wendy's eyes opened groggily. What a dream. All she could think of was whiteness, glowing in the dark. Then she felt the breeze on her face coming from her open window and remembered the breeze high up at Belvedere Caste.

She got up to brush her hair and spotted her moon key outside of her shirt. Her face lit up as she relived the events of the previous night. Her initiation! Excitedly, she examined the silver charm in her mirror. She looked and looked. She even took it off. There was no tiny diamond.

Chapter Seventeen

That day, Wendy took the boys to explore Central Park. She had to see for herself. Sure enough, they found Belvedere Castle just as it had been last night at LATCH. The boys loved climbing all over it and sword fighting like knights of old. When she finally got into bed that night, she was drained. Thoughts whirled in her head about the Moon Mystifier, the Statue of Liberty, Phillip, April and her missing diamond star. She fell fast asleep, assuming that after so much activity, they would have a night off.

Wendy's head jerked off her pillow. She was sure that she heard a rustling on the fire escape. Her clock said 11:55 PM. It was Pedro.

Pedro winked at her. "How does it feel to be a New Moon Member of LATCH?"

"It feels great, but I . . ."

". . . have a few questions." Pedro finished her sentence. "I came early, 'cause I thought you would."

"When I looked at my moon key this morning, there was no New Moon diamond."

"That's right. The diamond stars are only visible when we're at LATCH. During the day, they seem to disappear. That's so you won't have to answer a lot of questions."

Wendy smiled in relief.

Pedro asked, "How did you feel about the Moon Mystifier images?"

Wendy's smile disappeared. "I hate how other people see me. I look so unhappy. I *am* so unhappy—or at least I was until LATCH started." Wendy's voice dropped. "I don't really have any friends at school. My best friends are the boys—Ralphie, Eddie and Joey, and they're five, four and two."

"Don't be too hard on yourself. Living with different foster families hasn't made your life easy. It's hard to make friends when you move a lot. You'll be surprised at how much LATCH will change your attitude toward life. You should have seen how little confidence Helena had at the beginning."

"She's so beautiful, I can't believe she was ever unsure of herself," protested Wendy.

Pedro cut in sharply, "That expression has to go."

"What expression?" Pedro's curt tone surprised her.

"*I can't believe*. The only way to accomplish anything in life is to believe that you can. Not believing sets up barriers and limits. All the great inventors, explorers, scientists, artists and leaders accomplished amazing things because they believed that they could. Part of Helen's beauty comes from the fact that she is happy with herself, with her accomplishments."

Wendy smiled. "Well, I know I'll never be gorgeous like Helena, but it's true that when I believed that I could make something of my life on my birthday, that's when I got invited to LATCH."

"Exactly," Pedro nodded. "I think we should get going . . ."

"One more thing," Wendy said in a rush. "What happened when Phillip looked into the Moon Mystifier and it went crazy?"

Pedro looked serious. "What happens between the Moon Mystifier and someone is personal. Obviously, Phillip has some issues to deal with. My best advice to you is the same as before. Let Phillip do his thing. You do yours."

Wendy gulped. If only she had ignored Phillip at the Statue of Liberty. Pedro took her hand, and they were off.

This time Wendy knew exactly what to do when they arrived at the gray doors. Proudly, she angled her necklace so that it caught the light just so. The tiny reflection darted on the surface of the door like a firefly. The keyhole materialized and the door swung open.

"We're back at the planetarium tonight?" asked Wendy.

"It's often where we meet for LATCH business."

Like last time, the circular room was a brilliant, detailed magnification of the moon. Wendy knew that the shadows were craters, mares and highlands, but they looked like giant free-form puzzle pieces. Wendy could imagine a leaping rabbit, a dancing clown, a spaceship. Every image suggested a story.

Pedro seemed to know what she was thinking. "People have stared at the moon for centuries and made up tales. The Hindus believed that the moon was the storehouse of the elixir of immortality. The gods drank the magic potion from the moon so that they would never die. That's why the moon got smaller and smaller until all the elixir was gone. Then it had to refill itself so they could drink again. That's how they explained the waxing and waning of the moon."

As they were talking, the floor opened up and Petavius and Diana appeared like they had last time. Diana motioned for them to sit in the circle of four chairs.

"Welcome, Wendy. We're here to plan your New Moon activities," began Petavius. "Did you enjoy your initiation last night?"

"I'll never forget it," Wendy whispered, a little awed.

"Why don't you tell us what you've learned about yourself from the revelations," prompted Diana.

Wendy thought about her various experiences. "Well, I've learned that I like structure and information. I've gone crazy not knowing what was happening all the time."

"Yes," agreed Petavius. "So you need to work on flexibility and risk-taking. What else?"

"I can't tell you how many people have told me to trust, to believe since I've started LATCH. April was the first one to get me to trust when we swam with the sea lions. I've always been terrified of water," Wendy confessed.

Wendy noticed Petavius and Diana glance at each other.

"We are all afraid of some things," murmured Diana. "But, as Winston Churchill said, 'The only thing we have to fear is fear itself.'"

Wendy continued shyly, "I've also learned some good things about myself. I can be brave when I'm protecting someone else, like the arctic fox with the polar bears."

"You were also very brave when you ended up in Phillip's painting as the enslaved king," Diana added.

"I was so mad. I wanted to break Marius in two. It was weird being in a man's body," Wendy remembered.

"Our bodies have a lot to do with how we feel, what we think we can do," noted Petavius. "That's why we work on improving physical stamina and prowess so much at LATCH. A strong body can help you be a strong person."

"I've never been very athletic," Wendy burst out.

"I think you'll find that your body is more than capable. With a little training and self-confidence you'll surprise yourself." Petavius was encouraging. "What about the third image in the Moon Mystifier, the Wendy you have the power to be?" he asked seriously.

Wendy's voice dropped to a whisper. "That person seemed like a fantasy. If I can become half that happy, I can't imagine anything better."

Petavius' face grew dark. "No, that's not good enough. You must realize your full potential. You must believe in yourself. That's why you're at LATCH. Anything less is unacceptable."

Wendy was frightened. She had never seen Petavius like this. Even Pedro looked surprised. Diana reached over and touched Petavius' hand. Wearily, he shook his head. "Now you see, I also have a temper. What upsets me the most in life is waste. Please don't waste all the wonderful talents you possess."

"I'll try," Wendy said.

She wasn't sure she could name any of her talents. Did Petavius mean her magic? Was she really as powerful as April and Phillip had suggested after the statue of Liberty revelation?

"Trying is the first step, but you must also *believe* that you can," Petavius repeated fiercely.

Wendy sat back in her chair. She was intimidated by Petavius' intensity. What if she couldn't live up to his expectations? She glanced at Pedro for support.

Diana took over. "I think your insights about your revelations are very valuable, Wendy. Petavius and I had come to similar conclusions. Therefore, we are recommending that your first year of work include Eclipse, Illumination, Cloud Counting and two nights of R and R."

"R and R two times a week?" Pedro asked clearly surprised. "She'll die."

"In this case, it's necessary," Diana responded firmly.

"R and R?" Wendy asked, totally confused.

"Rotations and Revolutions," explained Pedro. "That's how the moon moves. It's our LATCH name for our physical movement activity. If Hercules can't get you into shape, it can't be done."

Petavius said, "I will lead you in your exploration of transformation in Eclipse. As you know, during a lunar eclipse, the earth comes between the moon and sun, casting a shadow on the moon and transforming how the moon looks. I will teach you to transform yourselves."

Diana continued, "I will be your guide in Illumination, which works on your inner light of hope, trust, belief and confidence."

"Did you say Cloud Counting as well?" Pedro's tone was confused.

Diana cleared her throat, "We have a special situation when it comes to Wendy's training in concentration. Based on Petavius' recommendation, we believe she should attend Cloud Counting."

Pedro turned to Wendy, his eyes studying her intently. "Cloud Counting is a third-phase activity. I've never heard of a New Mooner attending C.C. You must really be good."

"I don't believe it will be too advanced for you, Wendy. But, if it becomes too challenging, you can certainly drop back to a lower level," Petavius said.

Wendy felt like her head was swimming. What had she gotten herself into?

Petavius pulled out a piece of round parchment paper. "Now, I'd like you to take a minute, look at the moon, and then write down who you would like to be. The sky is the limit, pun intended." Petavius smiled. "Think big. If you could do anything, be anyone, what would you choose? It will be completely confidential, so don't be embarrassed."

Staring at the giant moon, Wendy thought of her most secret dreams. She got a picture in her mind. Suddenly her fingers were flying.

Wendy handed him her paper. Without looking at it Petavius folded it and sealed it into an envelope. "This is for you alone to open at the appropriate time. In the meantime, I will keep it in my treasure chest of hope."

As if on cue, the doors in the back of the room slid open. It was time to leave. Wendy was halfway up the aisle when she stopped. "Can I ask one more thing? Will Phillip be in many of my activities?"

Petavius answered, "You will have some crossover, but not every night."

That was something. "Thank you," Wendy murmured. "Good-bye." Wendy was temporarily blinded as she came out of the room, so she didn't notice Helena and Phillip right away.

"What did you tell him?" Phillip hissed. "I heard you say my name."

"I just asked if you'd be in my activities," Wendy said.

"What are you in?" Phillip snapped.

Wendy struggled to remember. "R and R, Eclipse, Illumination and Cloud something."

"Cloud Counting? That's a Half Moon activity." Jealousy flared in Phillip's eyes.

"They're waiting for us, Phillip. Let's go focus on your program," Helena coaxed as she dragged him into the room.

"Boy, you make him nuts, don't you?" whistled Pedro. "Well, at least you can be sure he won't be in Cloud Counting with you and me. And I doubt he'll be in two nights of R and R. He's in pretty good shape."

Wendy winced. She knew that Pedro didn't mean to hurt her feelings. But she felt self-conscious about needing to take so much R and R. She'd never had a chance to do much exercise.

"So, that makes two nights without Phillip. You'll just have to see how it works out on the other three."

Wendy rolled over in the morning light. Something about the number three was making her anxious. Gradually, she came to consciousness and remembered what had happened. A feeling of dread washed over her as she remembered what the three meant. Three nights of Phillip. It was better than five. She prayed that April would be with her those nights.

Chapter Eighteen

Wendy picked a time when the boys were all watching TV to call April at Lucky Moon Dry Cleaners. She hoped she wouldn't get her into trouble.

"Wendy? I'm so glad you called. What are you taking?" April burst onto the phone.

"Two nights of R and R, Eclipse, Illumination and Cloud Counting," Wendy answered in a rush.

"Cloud Counting? What's that?" asked April.

Wendy was self-conscious. "I guess it's a third phase concentration activity. What about you?"

"R and R, Eclipse, Illumination, Moon Gazing and Reflection."

Wendy groaned, "We've got two different activities."

April said, "I just hope we're in Eclipse together. Adam says it's a great experience."

"I just hope we have our first activity together and I don't end up in Cloud Counting with the older kids before I have a clue how things work," said Wendy.

"You'll be fine. Uh oh. My uncle's glaring at me.

Gotta go." April hung up abruptly. Wendy continued to stare at the phone, lost in thought.

"What's Cloud Counting?" came a small voice.

Wendy whirled around. Joey was standing in the doorway. Wendy felt her face turn red as she scrambled for an answer. "It's a game," she stammered.

"Can I play, too?" Joey was excited.

"Well, the thing is, you have to count the clouds that cross the moon, and you'll be asleep," she improvised.

Joey wasn't going to let that stop him. "I'll stay up."

Wendy realized that she had created a monster. "We'll see."

The boys wanted to play "cloud counting" all night, but at last, Wendy got them to bed. She had to admit, though, that the game she had invented had been a lot of fun. The shapes of the clouds and the shadows on the moon had triggered the boys' active imaginations.

Bong, bong, bong, bong . . . Wendy didn't think that she had fallen asleep, but there was Pedro.

In a blink of an eye, they were standing on a gigantic stage. It seemed as big as a football field. Wendy looked up and almost got dizzy. She had no idea that the space above a stage was so high.

"We're backstage at the Metropolitan Opera at Lincoln Center, where some of the best operas in the world are performed. A pretty cool place for R and R, isn't it?" Pedro smiled.

"I thought we'd be on a field or in a gym," said Wendy.

"Hercules has some interesting ideas about how to train people. Have fun." Pedro turned to go. "See you later this week in Cloud Counting."

Pedro waved good-bye and Wendy panicked. She was so scared that her legs felt weak. She sat down on the floor.

"Tired already?" intoned a familiar voice. "I figured you'd be here since you're in two sessions of R and R," Phillip sneered. Wendy's worst nightmare was coming true. Here was Phillip with no April in sight. "Luckily, I work out every day, always have," he bragged.

"I'm sure this class will be a piece of cake for you, won't it, Huntie? I'm surprised they didn't ask you to take over. Maybe we should tell Hercules that he's not needed." April appeared, ready for a fight.

Before anyone could answer, the lights dimmed and a blinding spotlight flashed on something or someone who was soaring over their heads. A muscular man dressed in a leopard skin with his hair in a ponytail landed on the stage in front of them with a thump. "I'm Hercules," he said with a grin. "Did I just hear that someone else wanted to lead this activity?"

No one answered. Phillip flashed a hateful look at April.

"Very well. Welcome to Rotations and Revolutions, named for the moon's rotation on its axis and revolution around the earth. FYI, I am not named for the cartoon character, but rather for the very brilliant crater on the northeastern quadrant of the moon, which was named for the Greek god.

"Everything that you've heard about this activity is untrue." The group let out a collective sigh. "It's worse, much worse," he said, flashing a devilish grin. "But I promise you, you will never feel better about yourself."

And with that, the lights changed and music floated into the giant space. Hercules led them through a series of stretches. Wendy realized that she was as tight as a drum. "Okay, let's begin our warm-up," announced Hercules. Wendy's eyes popped open; she was already exhausted.

"A lap around the main floor and the mezzanine, up to the top of the stage grid and back here," Hercules ordered.

Most kids ran off to the seating area. April grabbed Wendy's hand. "Let's do the lap backwards and go up to the grid first."

Wendy scrambled behind April without thinking as they climbed up and up. At the sixth level they were even with the huge poles that held the scenery. They seemed miles above the stage, but, there was one more level. Her legs trembling, Wendy forced herself not to look down. Now they were right under the ceiling, by the motors that raised and lowered the scenery. All she needed to do was follow the catwalk around the back and down, and she'd be fine. She vowed she could do it.

April moved quickly to the other side, out of sight.

"Hello, Wendy." Phillip appeared from nowhere.

"Phillip, please let me by," Wendy mumbled frantically, trying not to look down.

"Oh, look. Hercules is waving at us," Phillip said, pointing down.

Reflexively, Wendy's eyes darted down toward the stage. Immediately, she felt dizzy. Hercules was nowhere in sight.

Phillip tried to cover his snicker. "Sorry, he just moved off. Guess he wasn't waving at us after all." Phillip's ruse had worked. Wendy was paralyzed with fear. "You've got to have a strong head to survive at LATCH," he mocked as he moved off quickly.

Wendy sank to her knees. She couldn't do this. She

might as well drop out now. Time passed, Wendy stayed curled in a ball, every muscle tensed.

"Wendy, what happened?" April must have realized Wendy was no longer behind her and come to find her.

"Phillip," Wendy whispered.

Furious, April instantly understood that Phillip had done something to scare Wendy. "I'll get you down. I won't let you fall. Trust me."

The absolute certainty of April's voice seemed to unfreeze Wendy. Slowly, she began to crawl, like a baby. By the time they finished, the rest of the group was waiting for them on the stage. Everyone clapped when they finally arrived. Wendy was mortified. Phillip just stood there as if nothing had happened.

"Now I'd like to get a better idea of what level everyone is starting at," Hercules said. He motioned them to a large round mat at the back of the stage. One by one he asked them to move any way they liked. Of course, Phillip showed off with a series of professional looking karate kicks, basketball dribbles and tennis serves. He finished with a neat back handspring. April moved gracefully in a beautiful Korean dance. When it was Wendy's turn, she was so self-conscious that she almost fell down as she tried to twirl like the moon. She could see that Phillip was biting his lip to keep from laughing out loud.

"We're going to try something different," Hercules announced. "You are now going to play the Three Musketeers. Choose your outfits and swords in the wing off stage right."

Laughing, the group raced to the racks of elaborate costumes. Wendy was determined to do better at this exercise. She chose a brilliant red brocade jacket and a hat with a red plume. To match her outfit she picked a gleaming sword with a red tassel. Holding it, she felt like a new person.

After demonstrating some moves, Hercules paired them off so that two musketeers faced each other. Wendy was used to playing knights with the boys. She knew what to do. The pairs rotated around. Wendy began to relax. And then, her opponent changed. Her eyes met Phillip's.

"I've fenced for years," Phillip informed her as he lunged at Wendy. Quickly, Wendy parried and avoided Phillip's sword, surprising him. Before he could react, Wendy lunged back, knocking off his hat.

This seemed to make Phillip mad. His eyes narrowed and he came at Wendy. But no matter which direction he stabbed at her, she was always there first, blocking his blade. "You've fenced before," he snarled.

"No, I haven't," Wendy answered truthfully. Goofing around with the boys really didn't count.

Hercules was staring at them when he clapped his hands. "Let's move on. Who has always wanted to fly?"

Without hesitating, Wendy shot her hand up, "Me!"

Hercules looked surprised. "Excellent. Come with me." Hercules strapped on a special flying harness and clipped her onto a wire. One minute, she was standing on the stage and the next she was soaring high above it. At first, she panicked. But soon she began to feel like a bird.

She was laughing from the pure enjoyment of the experience when a roaring wall of flame appeared in front of her. She couldn't stop her forward motion and swooped through it, expecting the worst. But, it didn't burn her and suddenly she burst through to the other side. As the brilliance of the fire died away, Hercules emerged opposite her.

"En garde," he called, raising his sword. The match had begun. Feeling like she was in a fantasy, Wendy dueled with Hercules. They swooped at each other, sometimes missing, sometimes clashing swords. Wendy was never quite sure how she was controlling her movement. It seemed like she could just think of where she wanted to be and she'd be there. Wendy noticed Hercules looking away for a moment and flew toward him. Surprising everyone, but mostly herself, the clang of her sword knocked his sword out of his hand. It went clattering to the floor.

Hercules looked stunned. Then he started clapping. "Bravo." Wendy felt a surge of triumph and then in the same second, she felt sad because the game was over. Slowly, they sank down to the stage.

"All of our activities at LATCH are linked together," explained Hercules to the group. "This exercise involved movement, concentration and transformation. You see what happened when my concentration lapsed. I lost my sword."

Everyone started begging to go next, but Hercules said, "All of you will get your turn. But we're done for tonight. Get a good night's sleep."

April came up to her. "You were great." But before Wendy could thank her, April started vanishing. "Bye . . ."

Wendy looked around and realized that she was the only one left standing on the stage.

"I let everyone else go, because I wanted to talk to you," Hercules said.

Wendy assumed the worst. "I'm sorry I knocked your sword down."

"Are you kidding? That was great. You are a natural flyer. It's a rare day when a New Mooner gets my sword. When I was just starting, there was this girl . . ."

Wendy flushed with pride. She wondered why she was good at such odd things and so bad with everyday life.

"Do you understand what happened here tonight?" Hercules asked.

Wendy shook her head.

"You were a disaster for the first half of the night—awkward, stiff and clumsy." Wendy winced. Hercules continued, "Then you put on that silly red costume and you became a magnificent musketeer. Why did that happen?"

"I don't know." Wendy felt terrible.

"Because Wendy Hilton is a mess," Hercules explained matter-of-factly. "She thinks the worst about her body. But as soon as the same mind inside of Wendy's body is given permission to fly free as someone else, such as a bold musketeer, she has no limits! That same body can do things that it could never do as Wendy Hilton."

"That's true," Wendy had to admit.

"So our work is quite simple, and it's really much more about your mind than your body. We have to convince your mind that it doesn't have to be someone else to be powerful and unlimited. Of course, it won't hurt to strengthen your muscles and increase your stamina while we're at it. Now go home and rest up. You're going to be sore."

"Can I ask you one more thing? What was that wall of fire? Why didn't we burn?" Wendy asked.

"Remember what Petavius said at orientation. Everything is not what it seems. That was a piece of stage magic that they use for the opera. The flames were being projected on a wall of steam that rises up from little holes in the stage floor. It looks incredibly real, but instead of getting burned, you just get a little damp."

Wendy looked down at the floor and sure enough, there was a row of little holes.

Bong, bong, bong . . . The bells finished tolling midnight. Already, Wendy was fast asleep with a little smile on her face. Her right hand was curled up, as if she was holding a sword.

Chapter Nineteen

Once LATCH started, it started with a bang. There was no more waiting between sessions. The second night Wendy was still sore from Rotations and Revolutions when she arrived at the Big Apple Circus tent. It was filled with trapeze equipment, giant rolling barrels, and all kinds of colorful props. Wendy assumed it must be her second R and R class. But it was Diana who appeared in the center of the ring welcoming them to Illumination. Again, April and Phillip were in the group, along with half of the New Mooners.

Diana started them on the tightrope. One by one, every one of them fell off, until Diana suggested that they close their eyes and picture themselves balancing as they moved along the tightrope. When they did, they were amazed that they could actually manage a few steps.

Luckily, Phillip stayed away from Wendy and she had a wonderful time working with April. The nature of the class was much different than the night before. They didn't race around with crazy music.

They worked by themselves or with one other person developing belief, trust and confidence.

The next night Wendy was swept off to a place she had never heard of before, the Cloisters. It was a special medieval museum set high over the Hudson River in upper Manhattan. Their teacher was a very old woman named Persephone. She had waist-length curly gray hair, which hung loose down her back.

Wendy was intimidated to be with the Half Mooners. The fact that Pedro was there, however, made it a little easier. And Helena couldn't have been nicer. Wendy wished she could ask Helena what was going on with Phillip.

Persephone had a gravelly, somber voice. "Of course, each of the leaders at LATCH believes that his or her activity is the key to success at LATCH and life." Her eyes twinkled with mischief. "But I am the oldest, and naturally the wisest, and I happen to know that if you can master concentration, you can master anything."

And then she led them through a series of the most curious exercises. There was none of the madness of R and R with its lights and music or the colorful environment of the Big Apple Circus. The Cloisters was a large stone complex filled with ancient furniture and artwork. It had a hush about it, almost like a church.

Since it was a warm evening, Persephone had them lie outside and look up at the moonlit sky. She asked them to count the clouds that passed over the moon. Although the challenge appeared very easy, it was difficult not to let your mind drift off. Wendy lay there tickled that the game she had invented for the boys was so similar. In the time given, Wendy counted twenty-six clouds, the same as Persephone.

The next exercise was counting the different kinds of flowers in the unicorn tapestries. After staring at the tapestries for a long time, the unicorn seemed to come alive. Wendy was absolutely convinced that she had seen him blink, but she didn't say anything.

When they were warmed up, Persephone announced that they were ready to pick up where they had left off last year. Pedro groaned, "I'm terrible at this." Persephone demonstrated how she could concentrate on a candle from across the room and make it burst into flame. She split them up into two teams for Candle Tic-Tac-Toe.

Nine candles were arranged in three rows like a tic-tac-toe board. As a group they would concentrate on the candle they wanted to "play." Wendy thought it sounded impossible. But, sure enough, when they all concentrated together, a finger of fire would appear. Wendy's team won several games. The other team had trouble getting the right candle to light.

After the game, Pedro said, "I hope you're always on my team. We never did so well last year."

Wendy woke up the next morning with dreams of riding a unicorn in the moonlight. She hadn't wanted the dream to end. She had missed April last night, but it had been nice not to have to look over her shoulder and wonder what Phillip was going to do to torment her next. She figured she had a fifty-fifty chance of seeing him tonight, since all she had left was her second R and R and Eclipse.

The fourth night Wendy arrived on the pitcher's mound in Yankee Stadium. Although it was the middle of the night, all the lights were on at the stadium as if there was going to be a big game. Wendy could feel the energy that surrounded her from all the past Yankee World Championship teams.

Neither April nor Phillip were there. When Hercules parasailed in from the upper deck, Wendy knew she was at R and R. They each put on a Yankee uniform and stretched as the organ played, "Take Me Out to the Ball Game." Then they ran around the field and through Monument Park.

Finally, out of breath and exhausted, they gathered back at the mound. Hercules made the announcement that Wendy was dreading. They were going to play a game. Wendy felt sick. She was a terrible baseball player. She couldn't throw a ball or run. She was always picked last for the teams in gym.

Wendy's team won the toss and decided to bat last. They all scampered onto the field to take their positions. Wendy hesitated, wondering where she could do the least damage. As a result, she got the position that no one else wanted: catcher.

Hercules was pitching for both sides. Wendy dropped his first few warm-up pitches. Then the first batter came up. He smacked a double. The second batter swung and missed at three straight pitches, but Wendy didn't catch strike three and the batter was able to advance to first.

That's when things went from bad to worse. The next batter singled and as the first runner was stampeding toward her at home plate, Wendy flinched and the ball skittered away. Before Wendy's team ever got to bat, the other team had scored eight runs.

Wendy felt like crawling under a rock after that inning. Hercules came up to her between innings and asker her what was wrong. She was dressed like a

Yankee, she should act like one. He pointed out that it was just the same as being a musketeer.

Wendy protested that this was different, because she knew that she couldn't play baseball. The other night, she hadn't known that she couldn't fence. Wendy spent the next few innings trying to convince herself that she was a mighty Yankee. But it was hard, after all those times she had been ridiculed at school. After striking out twice, she finally managed to get on base with a bunt. Her team lost 24–5.

Afterwards, Hercules talked to her again. "You know, tonight was a fantasy just as much as the other night. You could have hit one out of the park, just like Mickey Mantle or Derek Jeter. Lots of the kids did."

"I know that, but I couldn't forget who I am," Wendy admitted.

"Ah," replied Hercules. "That's exactly what we're working on, isn't it?" He paused. "Who are you?"

Wendy woke up sweating. The sharp crescent moon was etched in the sky. The clock read 2:30 A.M. Hercules' last question reverberated in her ears. Who was she? She was still dumpy, shy Wendy Hilton, the foster child. A few crazy dreams weren't going to change who she was overnight. She wondered if they ever could.

Chapter Twenty

"What's wrong, Wenny?" Concern filled Joey's four-year-old eyes. She had been snapping at the boys all day.

"Nothing. I'm just a little tired," Wendy answered as she pushed the stroller home from the library. The truth was that she was anxious because last night at LATCH had reminded her of her real life at school. For a while this summer, she had been fooled into thinking that she was becoming a completely different person. But she was no different. And the start of school was around the corner.

The boys settled down to watch afternoon cartoons. Wendy went to her room and her heart skipped a beat. Shadow was rolled in a soft furry ball on her pillow. Gently, so as not to startle the small creature, Wendy opened the locket.

Missed you the last two nights. I have Eclipse tonight, do you?
—*April*

Wendy smiled in relief. She had been worried about Petavius and his unpredictable moods. But with April there, she was sure she would be fine.

Wendy was too excited to fall asleep that night. It seemed like midnight would never come. The bells started tolling. *Bong, bong, bong, bong, bong . . .* Wendy frowned. Five times. She couldn't ever remember hearing the fifth chime.

Bong, bong . . . Now Wendy was certain that something was wrong. Maybe she was being dropped from LATCH. Maybe LATCH was not being held that night.

Bong, bong . . . With a whoosh, Wendy arrived in the middle of a noisy group.

"Oh, there you are, thank goodness," April ran over to greet her. "You were so late."

"The transportation part of LATCH bugs me. I don't like the fact that I don't understand it and can't control it," Wendy complained.

They were standing in an enormous high room with sound reverberating off of marble walls. Next to them was a small booth with four gold clocks on top. When they looked up they both gasped. Above them was the most brilliant blue ceiling, like the sky scattered with gold stars that formed constellations.

"I know where we are," April said excitedly. "We're at Grand Central Station, where all the trains go in and out of New York City."

"Where is Petavius?" Phillip demanded. Wendy turned around. In her joy at seeing April, she had forgotten that Phillip was likely to be there. "So how was your *second* R and R?" Phillip asked with malicious delight.

"Great. We played at Yankee Stadium." Wendy made it sound good.

Even Phillip couldn't hide his envy. "Hit any home runs?"

Wendy was furious. How did Phillip always know exactly how to get to her?

"Excuse me. Could you spare some change?" A feeble old woman wrapped in frayed blankets limped up to them.

Phillip turned away from the woman. "Sorry. I have no money."

Wendy doubted that was true. Wendy dug in her shorts pocket hoping that a coin might have stuck there from the grocery shopping. She was surprised when her fingers touched something hard. She was even more surprised when she pulled out a silver dollar. Where had that come from?

The woman admired it. "Oh my. I haven't seen a silver dollar in a long time. That must be your lucky charm."

Wendy wondered if it was lucky. She thought how the boys would love to see it. But when she looked into the woman's bright eyes, she realized that she didn't need this coin, lucky or not. She had her moon key. She had been initiated into LATCH. That was all the luck she needed.

Wendy held out the coin. "I'd like you to have it."

Slowly, the woman took the coin. If Wendy had blinked, she would have missed it. But as the old woman turned away, her gnarled back straightened, she threw off the blankets and she became . . . Petavius!

"Thank you, Wendy," Petavius said in his crone voice. "Welcome to Eclipse, everyone. As you just saw, Pet as you know him was eclipsed and replaced by someone else. That is what you are all going to learn to do in this transformation activity. Now tell me. Why did you believe I was an old woman?"

They all contributed reasons. But the overriding factor had been the woman's crumpled, limping body.

"Exactly," smiled Petavius, "because of my appearance, the outside. So that is where we're going to begin." He led them to the upper balcony and instructed them to observe carefully every detail of the people crossing through the terminal.

Phillip cornered Wendy. "You think you're so smart giving that silver dollar to the beggar woman. But I know you were just trying to make me look bad. You knew it was Petavius all along, didn't you?"

Wendy stared at Phillip. If she told him that she had had no idea, he would never believe her anyhow. She turned on her heel and walked away.

"All right. Now, I'd like each of you to transform yourself into one of the people you've observed. The rest of us will guess who you are portraying," announced Petavius.

April started. She shoved her hands into her pockets while her eyes darted around furtively. Right away, everyone guessed that she was the shady man with the greasy hair and ripped shirt who looked like he was up to no good.

Several other kids took their turns. Wendy was curious who Phillip was going to be. Finally, he volunteered. His face had a haughty, distracted look. He kept his shoulders back, looked at his watch and raced for his train with purposeful, athletic strides. This was a man who believed in his importance.

Wendy thought that this man was exactly like Phillip. She wondered where the transformation part came in.

"That was fine, Phillip. You were very much like those executive commuters. But next time, I'd like to see you try someone really different from yourself," Petavius commented, mirroring Wendy's thoughts. "Your turn, Wendy."

Quietly, Wendy got up. With her eyes slightly down, she started moving around stiffly, picking up things, pushing something around.

Phillip called out impatiently. "You can start anytime, Wendy."

Wendy kept her eyes downcast as though she hadn't heard him.

Petavius cleared his throat with a little smile. "I believe Wendy has begun."

They all started guessing. But they couldn't remember anyone acting like Wendy. That's when April got it. "Wendy's doing the maintenance man who was emptying the garbage cans the whole time we were playing this game."

Wendy was relieved, but chagrined. "That's right. I guess I didn't really get him right."

Another girl spoke up. "I have to admit, I never even noticed that guy."

Petavius said, "The maintenance man was there. Sometimes, it's very useful to transform yourself into someone invisible, someone who attracts no attention. Learning to contain your energy and emotions is an exercise we usually do later in the course. Wendy just experimented early."

Phillip cast a disgusted look in Wendy's direction. He clearly resented the fact that Petavius favored her performance over his.

Next Petavius led them to the lower level of Grand Central, right outside of the Oyster Bar Restaurant. "I always bring my first Eclipse session here," he explained with a twinkle. He directed Wendy and April to stand facing two opposite corners with their backs to each other about twenty feet apart. He whispered something to April that the group couldn't hear. Far away from April, Wendy started laughing.

Petavius explained that they were at the Whispering Wall. Because of the arches, the sound traveled across the ceiling and then curved down to the opposite corner. You could whisper facing the wall, and the person twenty feet away could hear you perfectly.

"What a week," Wendy said. "How are we ever going to face boring, regular school?"

"I know," April agreed. "We've got to talk. Let's meet at the park again on Sunday."

Wendy was thrilled. "Could we meet by the sea lions? So much has happened since our first zoo revelation."

"As soon as I can get it set, I'll send Shadow or call," April said.

Wendy's eyes sparkled. "I'll be there."

Chapter Twenty-one

It took a few weeks for April to get away. Her parents always had something for her to do on the weekends. But, finally, late in August, Wendy got a note from Shadow and went to look for April.

April jumped up as Wendy arrived. "What's wrong with you?" April noticed Wendy's limp right away.

"I decided to walk around the reservoir, to get in shape," admitted Wendy.

April looked at Wendy's feet. "It's those stupid sneakers. They're too old." Just then, one of the sea lions shot past them in the tank. "There's Seaweed." April waved.

"How can you tell them apart?"

April looked at Wendy in surprise. "They're so different." The sea lions had gathered in front of them, taking turns flipping out of the water and barking. "They remember us and want us to go swimming with them now."

Wendy looked knowingly at April. "It's nice of you to include me, but I know that they want *you* to come in." April blushed, having been caught in a white lie. "Are you going in?" Wendy asked. She never knew what to expect from April.

"I'd probably get arrested. I told them that this was not the right time. I hope we'll come back during LATCH," April replied wistfully.

They tried to talk, but the three sea lions stayed right in front of them making such a racket that it was like a sea lion symphony. They seemed very excited about something. April clapped and put her face up to the glass tank. One of the sea lions came down to meet her on the other side of the glass.

"They were singing 'Happy Birthday' to Scooter," April explained. "She's fourteen years old today. I just gave her a birthday kiss."

The zookeeper came out to feed the sea lions and Wendy and April decided to move away to someplace quieter. Wendy let out a big sigh. "LATCH has been so wonderful this summer. It's been like a fresh start for me. Except for Phillip and my incompetence in R and R, I feel like I fit in. It's so different from school, where I'm an outcast. I think it's going to be even worse this fall, knowing how much better things could be."

April gave her one of her fierce looks. "Well, it's time for you to take charge and make it better. We're not working on transformation for nothing." April eyed Wendy's rumpled clothes and ugly sneakers. "The first thing we have to do is work on your clothes."

"My foster family gives me hand-me-downs. They don't have a lot of money for new clothes. In the past, I never really cared what I wore," Wendy confessed.

April studied Wendy. "You're already looking fitter." Her face lit up. "Why didn't I think of this before? I think I may have a solution." April looked like a cat who had swallowed a canary.

"What is it?" Wendy asked.

"You'll see."

Wendy tossed and turned in her bed. She couldn't believe how quickly the summer had zipped by. School started tomorrow. In a way, it had been easier when she had accepted that she was going to be invisible, have no friends, do her schoolwork and come home. Recently though, she had let hope creep in. It was all because of LATCH.

She was in better shape and walked around the reservoir at least once a week. She had her first true friend, April, not to mention Pedro and Helena. True to her word, April had hatched a plan to get her some decent clothes. It turned out that lots of people never claimed their clothes from the dry cleaners. After a year, April's family couldn't store them anymore, so they gave them away. Wendy couldn't believe the great jeans and cute tops that had been left. She also couldn't believe the size that fit her. She was at least a size smaller than she had been in June.

For the first time, Wendy hoped that this year would be better. What if it was the same though? What if no one talked to her? What if she was picked last for every team and ate lunch hiding in the bathroom, because it was too painful to sit alone in the cafeteria? That was the problem with hope. It gave you the desire to go after things. But it also set you up for disappointment.

Wendy stared at the crescent moon. It was just like her moon key. An encouraging curve. Like a smile in the sky. It made her feel a little better.

Bong, bong, bong, bong . . .

* * *

Wendy knew where she was right away this time. Eclipse was back in the great room at Grand Central Station.

"Back to school tomorrow?" Phillip taunted. Somehow he always sensed her sorest point. "The private schools don't start till next week."

"I guess you've got another week to figure out how you're going to cheat this year. It's important to keep up family traditions." April arrived with her eyes flashing.

"Some families have traditions and some families have dry cleaners, I guess," Phillip retorted.

April applauded. "Good one, Huntie. And which family ends up with their hands cleaner at the end of the day, do you think?"

Phillip walked away, no match for April's comebacks.

April took a look at Wendy's pale face. "You'll be fine tomorrow. You'll be the new you. Take your sister rock if you need some support. I'm definitely bringing mine."

Just as Wendy was smiling at that idea, Petavius stepped out of the information booth. "Tonight, I'm going to show you a secret weapon in transformation and persuasion. Who would like to be first?"

April's hand shot up. "I love secret weapons."

Petavius took April aside and spoke to her. Then, she moved to the center of the room. A harried businessman came flying through, obviously late for his train. April stopped him. "Excuse me, sir, could you tell me which train is going to White Plains. . . ."

The man cut her off. "Sorry, I'm late." He strode off.

Another man came rushing through. Again, April intercepted him. This time, she flashed an engaging smile at him. "Excuse me, sir, could you tell me which train is going to White Plains?"

The man smiled wearily back at her. "That's my train. We'll have to run to make it. Track Twenty-five."

"Thank you so much. But you better go ahead. I'm waiting for my mother," April smiled apologetically. He ran off.

Petavius gathered the group around. "So what happened?"

Phillip answered, "The first guy was a jerk. The second guy thought that April was cute."

"Is that what everyone thinks?" asked Petavius.

Nick said, "I think April was different the second time, so that guy took pity on her."

"I said exactly the same words," April noted.

Wendy thought hard. "April seemed friendlier the second time."

"Why?" Petavius pressed.

"She smiled," Wendy said without thinking.

"*Aha!*" exclaimed Petavius dramatically. "*That* is the secret weapon."

Smiling was the secret weapon? Wendy didn't entirely buy it.

Petavius had each student try it. Unbelievably, it worked. When they smiled, people were much more responsive. Petavius even had Wendy ask two people if she could borrow train fare. The first one, when she didn't smile, couldn't get away from her fast enough. With the second person, though, her nervous smile seemed to melt the grumpy man's heart. "Here," he said as he thrust a five-dollar bill into her hand.

Wendy's face broke into a full smile. "Thank you so much. If you give me your address, I'd like to send the money back to you."

The man blinked at the radiance of Wendy's expression. "That's okay. Just be more careful the next time."

The group gathered around Wendy to compliment her, except for Phillip. Wendy hated asking for money. But she had to admit that it had been a lot easier the second time.

Petavius took over. "I know that a lot of you think that LATCH is about impossible magic and mysterious lunar power. However, some magic is very easy to do. In fact, sometimes it's the most powerful of all. I want all of you to practice this technique at home."

Wendy noticed that everyone was standing there smiling like Cheshire cats. April turned to her. "Good luck, tomorrow." Before Wendy could reply, the rushing sound was in her head and she was back in her bed fast asleep.

Chapter Twenty-two

Wendy's fingers trembled as she put on her new jeans. It was only 6:00 A.M. She wouldn't be expected to get the boys up for half an hour. She thought of last night and tucked her sister stone in her pocket. That would have to bring her luck.

"Wendy?" a small voice whispered.

Wendy opened the door and there was Ralphie, completely dressed for his first day of kindergarten. "I'm scared," he whispered.

"You know what, Ralphie? Everyone will be scared just like you." Wendy searched for something to make him feel better. She had an inspiration. "But, just in case, I'm giving you my magic pebble." She pulled the small white rock out of her pocket. "I got it in a magical place. If you need some help, just rub it and it will make things better."

Reverently, Ralphie held out his sweaty little palm. "Thanks."

"It'll be our little secret. I don't think your brothers or parents need to know," Wendy added.

Ralphie was amazed. "We won't tell Joey or Eddie?"

"When they go to kindergarten, I'll give them the pebble, too."

Ralphie's eyes shone with pride at the special treatment.

Wendy found her new homeroom at I.S. 99. So far, nothing was different. No one talked to her. On the good side, no one seemed to be pointing and snickering at her, either. But she was still invisible.

She got her class schedule and her heart sank when she realized that she had gym first period. The teacher took them outside to play kickball. It was time to pick teams. Angela and Zachary, two of the most popular kids, volunteered to be captains and Wendy's nightmare began. One by one, they selected their friends. Wendy knew she was going to be chosen last. Her shoulders slumped. Her face sagged. She felt like crawling in a hole.

No! This was not going to happen. She thought of Hercules and everything she had learned at R and R. She took a deep breath and moved eagerly toward the captains. She picked up a ball and started to bounce it, as if she couldn't wait to play. Zachary peered at her, almost as if he didn't recognize her. "Wendy?"

Wendy remembered last night. Her secret weapon. She forced a friendly smile onto her face, "Hi, Zach."

It worked. "You're with us," he nodded. Triumphantly, Wendy joined the team. For the first time ever, she wasn't picked last. She held her own in the game. It wasn't like she was the star or anything, but she did manage to kick a double.

"Nice work," Zach grunted when the inning ended. For the first day, it was a start.

The rest of her classes were uneventful. And then there was lunch. She was standing at the entrance to the cafeteria when one of the girls who had been picked last at the kickball game came up to the doorway and stopped. Wendy could see that the girl looked more frightened than she was.

It was now or never. "Would you like to eat with me?" asked Wendy, remembering to smile.

"Oh, thanks. I'm new. I'm Hannah," responded the girl gratefully. They were just sitting down as Angela and her group came by. Wendy almost choked on her sandwich when Angela actually nodded at her and moved on.

She turned back to Hannah. She had curly dark hair that seemed to have a life of its own and interesting clothes. They weren't dumpy, but they weren't like the other kids' either.

"I like your jeans," said Hannah. Wendy silently thanked April.

"Thanks. I like your name," said Wendy.

"Me too," Hannah agreed. "It's the same spelled forwards and backwards."

Right then, Wendy was pretty sure that they were going to be friends.

Chapter Twenty-three

Wendy opened her window. A cool autumn breeze blew in. It was early October and Wendy had been doing double duty for several weeks now. She was so tired from going to school all day and to LATCH all night. Even though she got a full night's sleep, her days were twenty-eight hours long instead of twenty-four. And those extra four hours were packed with activity, especially on her R and R nights.

At least she was growing stronger. The other night Hercules had them run all the way up the steps of the Empire State Building. Diana was getting Wendy to try things that were unthinkable a few months ago. She had even swung on the flying trapeze. Eclipse was fun with April. Cloud Counting was Wendy's favorite, though. For some reason, she was pretty good at it.

There was a knock at her door. Ralphie was standing there in his pajamas. He looked very serious. "You can have this back. I didn't lose it." Lying on his palm was her sister stone.

"You can keep it longer, if you want," Wendy said.

Ralphie looked proud. "I don't need it anymore. I don't need the magic. Ever since the pebble helped me pick the winning name for our class rabbit, Captain Hook, the other kids have been real nice. . . ."

"I'm not so sure the pebble made you think of that name, Ralphie. Captain Hook has been your favorite character for a long time. Maybe you thought of it all by yourself," Wendy suggested softly.

Ralphie thought about that for a long time. Then his face broke out in a big grin. "Maybe," he agreed.

"You can have it back anytime you want," Wendy added.

"That's okay. Joey will need it next year." Ralphie turned to go.

Wendy's eyelids fluttered shut the minute she climbed into bed and off she went flying through the night to the familiar orange mound. Yankee Stadium looked different tonight. It had banners draped all over the stands. And then Wendy noticed something else special. It was a full moon.

"I've been wanting to come to Yankee Stadium," April said excitedly. "What's even better, it's decorated for the World Series."

"We already have our box seats, right behind first base," bragged Phillip as he came up to them.

"I have excellent seats, too," responded April seriously. "Right in front of my TV." Wendy and April broke out into laughter as Phillip walked away.

"Who does he think he is?" April shook her head.

"He's someone who can only feel good about himself by putting other people down," Wendy said.

Hercules sailed in from the upper deck in full uniform. "Six times around the stadium, and then get suited up."

Everyone groaned. "Six times around?"

The butterflies in her stomach were dancing a jig as Wendy put on her uniform. She remembered how awful she had been the last time they played baseball. And this time was worse. Phillip was there.

"Can anyone pitch?" asked Hercules.

"No problem," smiled Phillip, looking like he had been born in a Yankee uniform.

"I'd like to try," volunteered April. "But I've never thrown a baseball before." Wendy wondered if tiny little April could even get the ball over the plate.

"Okay," said Hercules. "I'll umpire. Pitchers pick their teams."

"I'd like Wendy," April called without hesitation. Wendy almost fainted.

"Are you crazy?" Wendy asked as she joined April.

"We're a team," April assured her. "I want you to be my catcher."

This was getting worse and worse. Didn't April know that she was the worst catcher in the world?

They flipped a coin and Phillip's team was up to bat first. April took the ball to the mound. And then an amazing thing happened. April wound up for a warm-up throw, and in a time-shattering blur, windmilled the ball over the plate. The ball was in Wendy's glove before she had seen April throw it.

"Ow," cried Wendy. Her hand was stinging.

Suddenly, Phillip wasn't looking so cocky. "I thought you said you've never thrown a baseball before!"

"I haven't, but I have thrown a softball," April added with a wink.

Phillip's eyes narrowed. This was war. April motioned Wendy to the mound. "You just concentrate as hard as you can on my pitches; they'll be over the plate and fast. I'll do the rest."

Wendy walked back to home plate convinced that April had lost her mind.

Nick was the first batter. April wound up and threw. Her first three pitches were balls. Phillip looked like he owned the world again. "Let her walk you, Nick."

Impatiently, April motioned Wendy to the mound. "You're not concentrating. Look at the ball and focus," she said sharply.

Wendy was upset when she walked back to the plate. April had never spoken like that to her before. She forced her eyes to zoom in on the ball in April's hand. It began to look bigger and bigger like the full moon with stitches. And then, it was in her glove.

"Strike one," called Hercules.

April flashed a big smile at Wendy and nodded. She readied for her wind-up. Wendy focused on the ball.

"Strike two."

Phillip was furious. "Hit it," he urged Nick.

Wendy's hand was vibrating from the velocity of the pitches. But she didn't take her eye off the ball.

"Strike three," called Hercules.

Nick was disgusted as he walked off. "I never even saw it," he said to Phillip.

April struck out the next batter and then Phillip came up. He was ready for revenge. Wendy was beginning to like baseball. It was much easier to just stare at the ball than to have to run and catch. She liked watching the seams rotate round and round. April threw her first pitch to Phillip. He swung for the stars.

"Strike one."

Two more times he missed . . . by a lot. It was all Wendy could do not to giggle. Maybe baseball could be fun after all.

And then, it was time for their team to bat. Phillip was so angry, the ball smoked by the first batter. Not to be outdone, he struck out all three batters.

And that's how it went, batter after batter. No one spoke. It was way too tense. Fifteen batters had struck out in a row when it was Wendy's turn to bat leading off the bottom of the third.

"Don't think about hitting it, just watch the ball," April advised. But Phillip threw three impossible curve balls. Wendy's bat never left her shoulder.

Next, it was April's turn. Fiercely, she crowded the plate, in no way intimidated by Phillip. After two swings, she managed to tip the ball into the catcher's mitt. Undaunted, April got her glove. "I'll get him next time."

But she didn't. For the next five and a half innings, Phillip and April struck out every batter up to the bottom of the ninth. A huge knot formed in the pit of Wendy's stomach. She was up.

"We're depending on you," hissed April. "Concentrate. I know you can do it."

April was nuts if she thought that concentrating was going to help her hit that ball. But there might be another way. Wendy cleared her head. Little by little, April, Phillip, Hercules and all the other kids faded away. It was just her and the ball. She looked up at the full moon and felt the full power of its magic.

Phillip started his wind-up. The ball came zooming toward her. She stared it away. It missed the plate outside by a fraction of an inch. "Ball one."

Wendy thought she might be getting the hang of this. After four more pitches, the count was three balls, two strikes. Wendy was exhausted. She stepped out of the box. Phillip paced on the mound, glaring at Wendy. She refused to make eye contact with him. She stepped back in, her eyes riveted on the ball.

This time the ball looked bigger than ever. It came toward her, faster, faster, heading for the center of the plate. With all her might, Wendy willed it to miss. Ten feet from the plate, it started to veer to the left. Inches from the plate, all the laws of physics melted away. The ball seemed to take on a life of its own. It cut away from the plate, almost hitting Wendy.

Phillip was stupefied. Hercules shook his head. "Ball four."

Wendy's team broke out in ecstatic cheers. Finally, a runner. Finally, some hope.

Phillip was like an enraged animal pacing around the mound when Hercules called, "Play ball."

With an effort, Phillip started his motion. Just before he let go of the ball, his eyes flicked to Wendy on first. She met his glance. And then, the pitch seemed to slip out of his fingers as if it were in slow motion.

April waited and waited and waited. At the perfect moment, the bat became an extension of her body and made contact with the ball. *Bam!* Phillip doubled over in pain on the mound. April tore around the base path screaming at Wendy to run. It looked like it might be a home run until the sailing ball tailed off in center field and hit the top of the wall.

"Run, run!" screamed April as Wendy raced home.

Nick heaved the ball to Phillip, who was waiting in front of home plate. Wendy's lungs were burning. Gasping, she started to slide as Phillip caught the ball and lunged at her for the tag. Wendy's foot slid across home plate just as Phillip smacked her on the thigh.

There was a stunned silence as everyone waited for Hercules to make the call. "Safe. Game over. April's team wins."

Phillip's angry face was right over Wendy's. "I know you did that. I'll get even with you," he hissed and stalked away.

Hercules smiled. "Great game. Some of the best pitching I've ever seen. Some of the most unusual pitching." His eyes slid to Wendy. "Petavius asked me to announce that the Blue Moon Ball is going to be held on Halloween for all phases of LATCH. Start thinking about your transformations now."

The game forgotten, everyone started talking about Halloween. April moved to Wendy.

"Thanks for believing in me," Wendy murmured.

"Are you kidding? Especially with the full moon tonight, I knew that you were the key."

"What do you mean?"

April rolled her eyes. "Don't you understand anything about yourself yet? There's a reason that you were skipped to Cloud Counting, a third-phase activity. I'm a pitcher on my softball team, and I'm good. But I'm usually wild. However, I figured with you catching that we had a chance. I knew you could make my pitches good. I just didn't realize how powerful you were. You even scored the winning run!"

"Only because you got that monster hit," Wendy said.

"Only because you had Phillip so rattled that he threw me a cream puff to hit. Ralphie could have hit a home run on that pitch." April's mind jumped to another topic. "Do you know anything about this Blue Moon Halloween Ball?"

"The only thing I know is that a blue moon refers to a second full moon that happens in the same month. It only occurs every couple of years."

April smiled. "Halloween and a blue moon. Imagine what could happen with that combination. . . ."

For some reason, Wendy shuddered and thought of Phillip. If her run-ins with him seemed to peak during a normal full moon, what could happen during a blue moon?

Chapter Twenty-four

"I wish we knew where the ball was going to be held," sighed Wendy.

"What difference does that make?" asked April.

"I just think it might inspire me. I'm having a terrible time deciding who or what to be."

"You're over-thinking this," said April.

"No, I'm not. Going to a ball is a total fantasy for me. I never thought anything like this would ever happen to me. I want my transformation to be really special."

"No one's going to recognize me," April stated confidently.

"But you still won't tell me what your transformation is going to be, will you?" Wendy pressed.

April smiled smugly. "Of course not. That would spoil all the fun."

They were whispering on a break in Illumination. Suddenly, their twosome became a threesome.

"So, what are you going to be?" Phillip asked Wendy. "I see you as Cinderella *before* the ball, covered in ashes. Course, that wouldn't be much of a transformation, would it?"

"It would be like you coming as Henry the Eighth. Anyone crosses you, off with their heads!" retorted Wendy.

April giggled. "So, what are you going to come as, Huntie?"

Phillip's eyes gleamed. "You'll never guess."

Wendy thought of a million ideas. Nothing seemed exactly right, though. October was almost over, and she still had no plan. She was sitting in Social Studies day-dreaming, as usual, when inspiration struck. The picture just jumped out of her book. She got a tingling in her fingers. Somehow, she knew that this was the perfect transformation.

But would she be able to pull it off? She had no money. No resources. She'd need special clothes and accessories. How was she going to afford it? Then she had an idea.

Luck was with her. As she had hoped, R and R was held at the Metropolitan Opera again. The minute she arrived, Wendy knew that she had to act fast. When Hercules told them to take laps around the theater, Wendy ran backstage and headed toward the elevator.

"Hey, where are you going?" April called.

"Go away. I don't want to get you in trouble," Wendy whispered nervously. "Plus, I don't want Phillip to follow me."

"I don't know what you're up to, but I'm coming with you," insisted April.

The elevator arrived. "I've got to find some things

for the Blue Moon Ball. It's my only chance," Wendy explained.

Instinct, or something else, seemed to guide Wendy through the maze of the complex building. She located the wardrobe department. In a few minutes, she had found what she needed and stuffed the items into a shopping bag. "I hate borrowing these without permission, but I'll return them as soon as possible," Wendy told April. "Don't you need anything?"

April gave her a sly smile. "Not for my transformation."

They raced back to the stage, out of breath.

"Where were you?" Phillip asked suspiciously. "I never saw you . . ."

He had probably been waiting high over the stage to terrify her again, Wendy thought.

"We took a different route this time," April said.

The last thing that Wendy had to worry about was getting the shopping bag to travel back home with her from R and R. As soon as class was over, she grabbed the bag and held on tightly. Sure enough, when she awoke at dawn, it was sitting next to her bed. Her heart was pounding. Step One completed. This transformation was going to be a challenge for her. She was going to have to use all the skills Petavius had taught her to pull it off.

Chapter Twenty-five

It was 10:00 P.M. when Wendy finally got the boys to bed after trick-or-treating. Between their costumes and all the candy, they had been bouncing off the walls. Wendy was completely wiped out. How in the world would she ever have the energy to pull off her transformation and attend the ball? She decided that the only thing to do was lie down and take a little nap. She'd rest for an hour. That would give her an hour to get ready.

It was 11:47 when her eyes fluttered open. Wendy almost screamed in disbelief. She must have slept through her alarm. She had thirteen minutes for her clothes, hair and makeup. She sprang off her bed and started her race against time.

The digital clock had barely clicked to 12:00 when Wendy was carried off in a rush of wind. She felt rattled and confused. She wasn't ready. How was she ever going to make her transformation work?

And then, she arrived. Somewhere. It didn't seem

like she was at any ball. In fact, she was all alone in what appeared to be a cave. It was a dark, small enclosure with no windows.

At first, Wendy felt as if she were blind. Then she realized a little light was trickling in from an opening somewhere. As her eyes adjusted, she could see that she was in a room made out of stone blocks. Where was she? Where was the Blue Moon Ball?

Wendy moved toward the light. At last, she could hear the low murmuring of voices. With all the concentration she could muster, she pushed away everything that had happened to Wendy Hilton in the last few hours. She wiped her mind clean, like an eraser on a blackboard, and filled it with images of the blazing sun on the desert and the shimmering water of the Nile. She imagined being the most powerful and beautiful woman in all of Egypt in 40 BC. She was twenty-nine years old and a queen. Wendy walked the last few feet and stepped out of the opening.

At that moment, the full moon moved out from behind a cloud, its radiance reflecting off of Wendy's blue robes, making it seem like she was in a spotlight. There was a gasp from the crowd. And then there was applause.

Wendy froze as she faced the group. As she feared, she didn't recognize anyone. There were flying angels, blinking robots and fire-breathing dragons. A huge snake slithered up to her and rose on his tail, as tall as Wendy. Wendy thought she should be afraid, but for some reason she wasn't.

"Good evening, Queen Cleopatra. Welcome to the LATCH Blue Moon Ball," the snake hissed. Wendy looked into the snake's wise eyes, and she instantly knew that the gigantic snake was Petavius.

She looked around and realized that she was standing in front of a pyramid. How amazing. But she wasn't in the desert. She was in a huge, glassed-in room, like a giant greenhouse. Then it came to her. She was at the Temple of Dendur in the Egyptian Wing of the Metropolitan Museum of Art.

"Good evening, Serpent," Wendy said, smiling her mysterious Cleopatra smile. And then something strange happened. The snake reacted to her voice as if she were a ghost. "Wendy . . . what a marvelous transformation. I had no idea it was you. And then, when I realized . . . it brings back such a flood of memories."

Before Wendy could ask Petavius more, a dashing Zorro came up to them.

Right away, Wendy knew who this was. "Pedro! It's Wendy."

Pedro was astonished. "Wendy? Impossible. You look so glamorous. I was sure you were Helena."

Wendy was delighted. "It's the costume."

Pedro studied her from head to toe. "It's much more than that. You're totally transformed. Especially your body. Double R and R has worked wonders. C'mon, let me introduce you around."

Petavius hissed at her. "We'll talk later."

As Pedro led Wendy across the crowded room, everyone complimented her on her transformation. Wendy could feel herself fill with confidence. What a wonderful sensation to be Cleopatra and to know that the whole world admires you.

An ancient, stooped-over hag came up to them. Pedro was at a loss. He didn't know who she was. Wendy stared at the decrepit woman. Then she thought about how she had picked her own transformation. "Helena?" she asked.

The hag stared at her and then burst out laughing. "Good work, Wendy. Fooled you, Pedro."

Wendy was pleased with herself. "I just tried to think of who was most unlike an old hag. You look unrecognizable."

Pedro eyed the two of them, "All I know is that both of you have a great shot at the Blue Moon Prize for Best Transformation."

"Isn't Petavius amazing as a cobra?" Wendy asked.

"He often chooses that transformation," said Helena. "It's sort of his trademark."

"How did you know we were going to be at the Temple of Dendur?" Pedro asked Wendy.

Wendy blanched. "I had no idea. We were studying Egypt in Social Studies. I saw a picture of Cleopatra and I just knew that's who I wanted to be. Have either of you seen April . . . or Phillip?"

"Haven't seen them," replied Pedro.

The music began. Amazingly, everyone wanted to dance with Wendy. She was the belle of the ball.

Wendy was catching her breath between dances, when Petavius appeared. "Could we talk for a moment? In private?"

Petavius led her to a shadowy area behind the temple. "The reason that I reacted the way I did when I realized that you were Cleopatra tonight is because you reminded me so much of another LATCH student who came as Cleopatra many years ago. It is uncanny. She came in a blue gown much like yours. Her name was Serena. She was a very gifted student, a lot like you. Extremely intuitive with exceptional concentration."

Why was Pet telling her this?

"And you see . . ." Petavius was interrupted by a loud fanfare.

Diana's voice echoed through the room. "And now it is time to award the Blue Moon Prize. Petavius, could you please come to the microphone. . . ."

Petavius looked frustrated. "We'll finish this later."

Petavius slithered off. Wendy was left in the shadows, confused. Two green eyes glowed in the darkness. The black and charcoal cat came up to Wendy and wound through her legs.

Suddenly, Wendy felt even more confused. She scooped up the small, familiar cat. "April, is that you? Have you come as Shadow?"

The cat looked back at her, unblinking. "Meow."

Just when Wendy had begun to feel comfortable with the unbelievable notion of LATCH, it seemed like the whole world was being turned upside down again. This evening had been so strange.

Diana's words cut through her thoughts, ". . . the Blue Moon brought out the most powerful transformations we have ever seen."

Wendy could hear Petavius and Diana list a series of students who deserved recognition, including Helena Huntington.

"But the person who transformed the essence of herself in the most dramatic fashion is . . . Wendy Hilton." Everyone started applauding.

It finally sank in. Wendy had won the Blue Moon Prize. But that was all wrong. "That's ridiculous," Wendy whispered to the cat. "Come with me and I'll tell them that you should win, April. Your transformation is nothing short of miraculous. You're as good as Petavius." Wendy started to walk to the front, but the cat wriggled out of her arms and vanished.

"Wendy, please come up here and accept your prize," Diana's voice persisted.

Wendy was in a daze when Diana placed a round

moon pendant on a black velvet ribbon around her neck. The crystal moon glowed with its own blue light.

"Congratulations!" A familiar voice got her attention. Wendy whirled around and there was April dressed as a cat, a human-sized black and grey cat.

Wendy's head ached, she was so confused. "Where have you been all night?"

"I've been here. We just missed each other."

Wendy grabbed April's wrist. "You can tell me the truth. You said no one would recognize you, because you became a real cat, you were Shadow. I saw you by the temple."

"I was by the temple at one point," April agreed innocently.

"April, you should have won," Wendy insisted fiercely.

"My transformation is nothing special." She indicated her black cat suit. "Anyhow, becoming a cat is not a stretch for me. People have always told me I was very feline."

Suddenly, something occurred to Wendy. The idea made her head explode. "Whenever Shadow has delivered messages to me, it's really been you, hasn't it? I've always wondered how a cat could find the way."

"Cats have a wonderful sense of direction. I told you I was good at training animals," April replied.

"Look, I guess you have your reasons for not telling me the truth. I'll have to respect that. But I know it was you," Wendy insisted stubbornly.

"I would never lie to you. You're going to believe whatever you want," April said. "I've got to go dance with Pedro. He's waving at me." And with that, April moved off.

Shaken, Wendy reminded herself that April was

the first real friend she had ever had. She had to trust that April had a good reason for not telling her the truth. Or maybe, Wendy was imagining the whole thing. Maybe that cat was just a cat.

Wendy spotted the giant cobra moving behind the temple. She needed to finish her conversation with Petavius. She followed the snake into the pool of darkness.

"Could we finish talking, Petavius," she asked, hardly daring to look at him. "That girl, Serena, who you told me also came as Cleopatra . . ." Wendy lifted her head to meet the snake's eyes and stopped. She had made a horrible mistake.

"You're not Petavius!" she gasped, looking into very different eyes.

"But I look like him, don't I?" hissed the snake proudly. "Everyone knows that Petavius often comes as a cobra. I thought it would be fun to come as one, too. Amazing what people have confided in me tonight. You do know that a snake killed Cleopatra?"

The voice told Wendy everything that she didn't want to know. "Phillip!"

"Surprise. Congrats on the Blue Moon Prize. Though, I can't say I'm surprised that Wendy Hilton, our star foster child, was in the perfect costume at the perfect place. The question is, why are you Petavius's pet?" Phillip's nasty eyes drilled into Wendy.

Wendy's fear changed into anger. "I know you won't believe me, but Petavius told me nothing about the ball. It was a total coincidence that I came as Cleopatra."

"You're right. I don't believe you. Petavius always has juicy little tidbits for you. The latest one seems to be about Serena . . ."

Wendy's stomach flipped. That conversation had been private between her and Petavius.

"Well, well, my long-lost brother cobra . . ." Neither Phillip nor Wendy had heard Petavius silently slide up to them. "I didn't realize that you had also come as a snake."

"Just a coincidence, I guess," Phillip said innocently, as he turned and slithered off.

"What was that about?" Petavius asked Wendy.

"In the darkness, I thought that Phillip was you, and I went up to him to finish our conversation about . . . Serena," Wendy explained uncomfortably.

Petavius's face was unreadable. "Serena is not a secret. Phillip's father attended LATCH with her. I'm sure he would have made the connection when Phillip told him about your costume."

Wendy waited. "But didn't you want to tell me something more about Serena?" she prodded.

Petavius hesitated for a split second. "I just wanted you to know that Serena went on to achieve great things at LATCH. I thought you would find that encouraging."

Wendy knew that there was more to this story. But, as always, Phillip had somehow wrecked it. "Perhaps, you'll tell me more about Serena another time?" Wendy pressed.

"Perhaps I will, if the time is right." Petavius' words promised nothing.

Suddenly, Wendy felt very weary. The whole evening had been too much for her. She wished she could be home in her bed. But she couldn't leave the ball until the backwards time reached midnight and she was transported home.

"At LATCH we try to introduce each of you to the unlimited power that is inside of you. If you want something badly enough and you concentrate, you can make almost anything happen." With a pointed look, Petavius moved off.

Wendy's thoughts were a jumble as she stood there. It was as if Petavius had read her mind. Was he telling her that she had the power to go home? She closed her eyes and concentrated on her bed. She willed herself to be there.

She was asleep before her head hit the pillow. It wasn't a peaceful sleep. It was sleep disrupted by full moons and snakes and shadowy cats and Cleopatras asking, do you know who I am?

Chapter Twenty-six

"I heard that Zachary's party was quite a happening," Hannah mentioned casually at lunch the next day.

Wendy sighed, "I wouldn't know."

"Stop protecting me. It's obvious that you're exhausted from a party last night." Hannah appeared certain that Wendy was lying to her.

"Look, Hannah, no matter what you think, Zachary would never have asked me to his party. I just had a really exhausting . . . dream." That was the closest to the truth that Wendy could come.

Hannah was interested. "What was the dream about?"

"Actually, I dreamt that I was at this amazing Halloween party. . . ." Once Wendy started, the details started spilling out. "It was at the Temple of Dendur."

Hannah's face lit up. "I've been there. Great place for a party. What else?"

"Well, at the beginning everything was fantastic. The costumes were incredible. There was dancing. But, little by little, everything got really weird. Nothing was as it seemed. A good friend came as a cat, a real cat. Two people came as cobras and one pretended to be the other one."

"Did the cobras talk?" interrupted Hannah.

"They hissed in words that I could understand," answered Wendy as she tried to remember how it had worked. It was such a relief to talk about it.

"Cool. Boy, the way you describe it, it seems almost real."

"That's the way it seemed in the dream."

"What was your costume?" asked Hannah curiously.

"I went as Cleopatra."

Hannah burst out laughing. "That's the most far-fetched part of your dream so far. You as Cleopatra?"

Wendy remembered winning the Blue Moon Prize. She smiled sheepishly at Hannah. "Yeah, it was pretty unbelievable."

Wendy was hurrying down the hallway after school when she bumped into Hannah. The shopping bag that Wendy was carrying hooked onto Hannah's bracelet and ripped the handle off.

"Hey, where are you going in such a hurry?" asked Hannah as she untangled herself and got a look in the bag.

Wendy snatched back the bag, folded over the top and carried it in two arms. "Gotta return something. Gotta go." Wendy hurried off with no further explanation. What would Hannah think if she'd spotted the black wig, sparkly blue fabric and bracelet in the shape of a snake in Wendy's bag. The perfect makings of a Cleopatra costume.

Wendy pushed open the doors at Lincoln Center and went up to the guard. "Excuse me. I need to return these things to the costume department," Wendy stammered. She held out the shopping bag.

"Well, you need to take them to the stage entrance," the guard told her.

"I'm sorry, but I'm in a terrible hurry." Wendy was beginning to panic. She wanted to get out of there. She forced herself to smile apologetically.

"Well, let me call up to the costume department . . ." The guard turned away to use the house phone. Quickly Wendy put the ripped shopping bag on his desk and left.

Wendy felt dizzy as she sat on the subway. The Blue Moon Ball had seemed so real last night. But the Blue Moon Prize necklace was not with her costume this morning. The whole ball had been so bizarre and unsettling. Hannah was right. It was totally unbelievable. In the cold gray light of November 1, it seemed impossible that it could have been anything more than a dream.

Chapter Twenty-seven

Despite the unusual magic of the blue moon, once it was gone, everything returned to normal. November was eerily quiet. LATCH activities continued as normal. Phillip seemed to be avoiding her. Petavius said nothing more to her. Wendy felt herself holding her breath, wondering what would happen next.

One night, after the first powdering of snow, the clock struck midnight and Wendy arrived breathlessly at the Wollman Skating Rink in Central Park. A crescent moon was etched in the crystal clear sky, making the snow sparkle like diamonds. True to LATCH, Wendy had arrived bundled in warm clothes with ice skates already laced on her feet.

Wendy had never set foot on ice before. Neither had a lot of the kids. Hercules didn't let that bother him. Within minutes, he had them skating around the rink. After a few nasty falls, Wendy got the hang of it.

April wobbled up to her side. "You're pretty good at this."

"I'm okay if the water is frozen," Wendy kidded.

They skated together side by side. "Have you heard about the holiday party yet?" asked April. "Kids were talking about it in Moon Gazing last night."

"At least we won't have to wear costumes," replied Wendy.

"Has Phillip tried anything since Halloween?" asked April.

"Nothing," commented Wendy as she spotted Phillip showing off in the center of the ice, doing jumps like a future Olympian. Was there anything that the boy didn't know how to do?

"I hear that he's been asking around if there are pictures of LATCH graduates anywhere," said April.

"He's still curious about why Petavius told me about Serena. I knew he wouldn't drop it," Wendy fumed. "If only I hadn't been so stupid. . . ."

"I wonder why Petavius mentioned her to you," April mused. "It's odd. He never singles me out."

"I think it was just the coincidence of our costumes," Wendy said.

"Probably," April agreed as she skated off.

At that moment, Phillip almost knocked Wendy over as he whooshed to a hockey stop right in front of her, spraying ice all over her face. "Wendy, I thought you'd like to know that Serena was supposed to be incredibly beautiful."

"Then, I guess, that's where our similarities end," Wendy retorted.

"Haven't you seen a picture of Serena?" Phillip fished.

"How would I have seen that?" asked Wendy.

"I figured that Petavius would have shown you one by now," Phillip said.

"I think you've got the wrong idea about this, Phillip. Petavius hasn't mentioned another word about her. It was no big deal." Even as Wendy said this, she wondered.

Hercules skated up to them. "Time for ice tag. Last one to the big tree is it."

Phillip started to push off. "You ever know someone at LATCH named Serena?" he asked Hercules casually.

Hercules answered without hesitation. "Sure. Everyone knows about Serena. I was a new teacher at the time. She was the star fencer of my class. She was so beautiful that every boy at LATCH was in love with her."

"Was she blonde?" Phillip asked.

"No, she had jet black hair and moon blue eyes," recalled Hercules.

Wendy didn't know why she was disappointed when she heard this. She made up her mind to follow her own advice and forget about Serena.

Chapter Twenty-eight

December flew by with all the usual Christmas madness. The boys were jumping out of their skin wondering what Santa was going to bring for them. Wendy even found Joey under her bed searching for hidden gifts.

"Joey, what are you doing?" she asked.

Caught in the act, Joey scrambled out from under the bed. "I was just looking for something," he defended himself. "I only found this old notebook."

Wendy quickly took it from him. It was her LATCH notebook. Luckily, Joey couldn't read yet. "Were you looking for Christmas presents?"

Joey flushed a telltale crimson. "I just wanted a peek. But I didn't find anything. I didn't find anything in my parents' room, either."

"You know you have to wait for Christmas morning," Wendy told him.

"But it's so hard."

"That's part of the fun of it."

"It's not fun for me," Joey protested.

"It will be."

Wendy tossed and turned that night, wondering what she would get for the boys. Joey's gift search had reminded her that she had shopping to do.

Bong, bong, bong . . .

At first Wendy thought that she was at R and R because she had arrived on a big stage that she assumed was the Metropolitan Opera. But as she looked around, she noticed differences. The theater wasn't quite as big. The chandeliers were different. The stage was decorated with a Christmas tree, wooden toy soldiers, life-sized ballerina dolls, giant stuffed mice and a big wooden nutcracker.

April bounced up to her. "So are you ready for the festivities?"

Wendy was confused. "What festivities?"

"The LATCH holiday party," April said.

Suddenly, someone came up from behind her and twirled her around. It was Pedro. *"Feliz Navidad,"* he said, grinning.

Without warning, the lights grew dim. Music started playing. April recognized it right away. "It's from the *Nutcracker* Ballet. This is where the New York City Ballet performs *The Nutcracker* every December."

Wendy closed her eyes and let the music paint pictures in her head. When she opened them, she thought something was wrong with her vision. Slowly, the Christmas tree was growing taller and taller and taller until it reached the top of the stage. The toy soldiers and mice had come alive. They were fighting. The toy soldiers, led by the Nutcracker, were capturing the Mouse King.

The music changed. Suddenly, a pale winter moon

appeared in the upper corner of the stage. Snow began falling. From behind the tree, the once lifeless ballerina dolls danced with the snowflakes, making patterns in the snow. The music built to a tremendous crescendo and the moon started to float across the stage. Someone was riding on the moon. It was Petavius.

Everyone cheered at the spectacle of Petavius riding his moon chariot through the sky. He glided down to the stage and stepped off, carrying a huge white sack.

"Happy holidays," he said. "First the gifts, then the party."

"I don't have gifts for anyone," whispered Wendy to April.

"None of us do, silly. How could we when we had no idea that the party was going to happen tonight?" April pointed out sensibly.

Petavius began calling out names. He gave each person a gift that resembled a small white cloud. There were no name tags on any of them. Wendy assumed that the gifts were the same for everyone.

"Wendy Hilton."

Petavius reached into his sack for her gift. As he was handing it to her, he suddenly pulled his arm back. He searched in his sack and pulled out another puff of white wisps. This time he smiled and handed it to her.

As Wendy moved back to her place, she noticed Phillip staring at her gift.

Everyone waited until Petavius had handed out all the gifts. All eyes were on him as he nodded. Excitedly, they ripped off the puffy covering.

The fluff came off in hunks. A little of it stuck to Wendy's fingers, and, without thinking, she put it up to her lips. The most delicious sweetness melted in her mouth. The gifts were wrapped in the best cotton candy that Wendy had ever tasted.

"Try it," Wendy insisted to April.

April looked at Wendy as if she were crazy. Then she tasted it. Soon the whole group was more focused on gobbling up their spun wrapping than what was inside. This was one party where there wouldn't be anything to clean up.

With all the candy gone, Wendy's gift lay in her lap. It was a small journal covered in dark blue velvet with a silver lock. On the front cover was a pearly white crescent moon.

Pedro showed Wendy his gift. "The Half Mooners get a moon magnifying glass." He looked at her gift and smiled. "Oh, the New Mooners journal. I remember that. Pet is big on writing in journals."

Wendy was surprised. Apparently, each phase got a different gift. With no name tags or obvious differences of any kind, Wendy wondered how Petavius could possibly have known how to give the right gift.

Pedro said, "I shouldn't spoil the surprise, but I don't want you to miss all the fun." He pointed to the crescent moon on the cover. "You can't tell in this light, but this moon glows in the dark, like the real moon. What's more, it changes phases just like the moon. Tomorrow it will be one phase larger."

Wendy was excited. "I can't wait to see it change."

Pedro laughed. "It's very slow, like the moon. You can't see it change by watching it."

They went to get some refreshments. A hand reached over Wendy's shoulder and grabbed her journal, startling her. "Let me see yours," Phillip said rudely.

Wendy whipped around. "What is your problem, Phillip? It's just like yours."

"I doubt it," said Phillip. "I saw Petavius pick a special gift out for you."

"Give it back," said Wendy, furiously. In the tussle, a small photo fell out of the book.

In a flash, Phillip had snatched it. It was a picture of a very beautiful dark-haired girl. "I knew it. It's Serena. It has to be."

Wendy's heart pounded. Why had that picture fallen out of her journal? Had Petavius meant it for her? "Why do you think this is Serena?"

"Because I think there was a reason that Petavius told you about Serena at the Blue Moon Ball. And now there is this strange picture in your journal. No one else had photos in their journals."

Why was this happening to her? Furiously, Wendy grabbed the photo back. It ripped in half as she pulled it out of Phillip's hand. "So what if it is Serena?"

Phillip pulled Wendy behind a wooden toy soldier. His face was inches from her. "Serena destroyed my father. My father, Phillip Huntington the Third, never finished LATCH because he had an accident caused by Serena. His political aspirations were ended. He has been a shadow of what he could have been because of her. I will not rest until Serena pays for what she did to my father, my family."

"I'm very sorry about your father. But I don't see what this has to do with me," Wendy sputtered.

"I'm not sure yet, either. But there's obviously a connection and I won't rest until I find it," Phillip said as he stormed off.

Wendy was trembling as she stared at the two halves of the dark-haired girl. Petavius had changed gifts to give her this one. She wondered if it could be

Serena. Thoughtfully, she tucked the ripped photo back into her journal. She was unsettled. Just like the Halloween Ball, this party had gone sour.

She looked for Petavius and found him surrounded by kids. This was no time to confront him. In any case, she wondered if he would even tell her the truth.

Wendy forced herself to go stand with Pedro and April. But, she could barely hold her cup of Sea of Nectar Punch, despite the fact that it tasted like gingerbread cookies tonight.

All she wanted was to go home, study the photo and make sense of the evening.

Chapter Twenty-nine

Wendy's head felt like it was made of fuzz when she woke up the next morning. That reminded her of the cotton candy wrapping last night. She smiled. With effort, she reconstructed the details of her LATCH evening. It was always hard to remember the next morning.

Her brow furrowed as she thought of her gift and Phillip and the ripped photo. Wendy searched the floor around her bed for her new journal. She checked everywhere. It wasn't there.

Wendy hated the fact that there was never proof of LATCH the next morning. She wondered what the point of a journal was that she couldn't use at home. It was probably like the diamonds on their moon key necklaces. They were only visible at LATCH. Wendy sighed. Just like her Blue Moon Prize. Or maybe she had made them all up.

Wendy suddenly felt so discouraged that she didn't know if she could get out of bed. Would she

ever really know if LATCH was anything more than a
dream? Pedro had told her long ago that they could
never be sure. To make matters worse, even if it was
just a dream, the dream was turning into a nightmare every time she encountered Phillip.

Finally, Wendy dragged herself out of bed. It was
Christmas Eve. She had shopping to do.

The cold day and the crowded stores did nothing to
lighten Wendy's heavy heart. She wished she could
talk to April, but she knew that April was busy with
her family today.

Wendy flopped down on a subway seat. She was
having no luck finding the action figures that the
boys wanted. The stores were picked over. She had
waited too long.

The subway car was completely empty except for
an old woman asleep in the corner. The woman's
handbag had slipped off her wrist in her sleep.
Wendy was worried. It would be easy for someone to
steal the woman's bag.

Trying not to disturb the woman, Wendy pushed
the bag back on her arm. But the bag just kept
slipping off. Wendy decided that she'd just have
to wake her. Ever so gently, she touched the
woman's shoulder. The woman's eyes flashed open
in alarm.

"I'm sorry to disturb you. Your purse was falling off
while you slept," Wendy said.

The woman protectively grabbed her bag and
searched it. When she realized that everything was
still there, her face broke into the most radiant smile.
"Thank you so much, my dear. That was very kind of
you. I hope you're going to have a very merry Christmas." Now that the woman was awake, she was alert

and vibrant. Her eyes seemed to encourage Wendy to talk.

"I thought this was going to be a wonderful Christmas. . . . But things have been happening. They've been ruining what started out so well. There's this boy who seems to hate me . . . I don't know what I did to him. . . ." Wendy knew that she wasn't making any sense. Her worries just came pouring out to this stranger.

Remarkably, the woman listened to Wendy's every word as if she understood perfectly. Nodding, she spoke in a soothing, supportive voice. "I'm sure you didn't do anything to him. What's making the boy hateful comes from inside him. Let him be. Proceed with your life. You seem like a special girl. I'm sure you have the strength you need. But just to help, I'm going to make a wish that you have a joyous Christmas, and that it's everything that you want it to be." The woman squeezed her eyes shut while she made the wish.

When she opened her eyes, they twinkled. She held her hand out to Wendy. "It's my stop. Will you help me up, dear?"

Wendy reached out. The woman's hand was comforting, warm and smooth. As the woman rose gracefully from her seat, she seemed light as a feather. Wendy didn't understand why the woman needed Wendy's help at all. Once she was standing, she continued to squeeze Wendy's hand. "A Christmas Eve gift to you," she said softly.

The subway came to a halt and the doors jerked open. The woman darted onto the platform and stood for a second smiling at Wendy. That's when Wendy felt it . . . in her palm. The woman's ring had slipped off into Wendy's hand.

The doors started to close. "Your ring came off!" Wendy called out frantically. She tried to lunge through the doors before they closed.

The woman smiled as the doors clanked shut. "Keep it, Wendy. I want you to have it," she called.

The train lurched to a start. The gold filigree ring was in the palm of her hand. It was warm and heavy with a small, round, milky stone. What had just happened? Should she keep the ring? She had no idea how to return it. Had she heard the woman right? Wendy was pretty sure the old woman had said that she wanted her to have it. Why would she give it to her? Maybe she was just a kind old lady who had lots of jewelry.

The train rattled along as a dazed Wendy replayed the incident over and over in her mind. Wendy was almost positive that the woman had said, "A Christmas Eve gift to you." She had smiled and told her to keep it. Wendy sat up straight in her seat. At the very end, the woman had called her by name! Wendy reviewed her conversation. She had talked about her worries. But had she ever mentioned her name?

Wendy's head was spinning as she got to her stop. She stared at the ring. The stone swirled with a pale, mysterious light. She couldn't help feeling thrilled. It was the first real Christmas present, other than practical clothes and school supplies, that she had ever received. It made no sense, but she felt that she was meant to have it.

Whatever the reason, Wendy's luck seemed to change. In the very last store that she checked late that day, Wendy found a box buried behind a Barbie doll display. It contained the action figures that the boys wanted. Wendy felt like she had found buried treasure. Now, if the old woman's good wishes only worked on Phillip, too.

When Wendy woke up on Christmas Day, she concentrated like she always did on what she had dreamed last night. But, she could recall nothing. It seemed that she had not been to LATCH during the night. She stretched, feeling relaxed and rested. She stared at her new ring.

Contrary to Joey's fears, the boys received piles of presents. Feverishly, they ripped open the paper, whooping with delight, crawling around the floor staging battles and adventures.

Wendy's action figures were the stars of the morning. The boys were wide-eyed when they opened them. Ralphie looked at her in awe. "My friends said these were impossible to get. The stores haven't had them for weeks."

"I got lucky," Wendy admitted, glancing at her ring.

Liz's eyes followed Wendy's. "What's that ring? Is it new?"

Wendy didn't want to lie, but she didn't want to tell the whole story, either. "I got it from a friend, for Christmas."

"It looks like a moonstone," Liz observed.

A chill ran up Wendy's spine.

"We got something for you, too," said Joey breathlessly as Ralphie presented her with a gift that the boys had obviously wrapped themselves.

Wendy looked at their three expectant faces. She wondered what in the world they could have gotten for her. She undid the wrapping. Inside was a diary with a crescent moon on an inky blue velvet background. Wendy's heart stopped. It was exactly the same as the journal Petavius had given to her at the Nutcracker party—her LATCH journal. She couldn't speak.

"Isn't it cool? Joey found it when we were at the discount store. It was the only one at the very bottom of a whole bunch of books. We knew you would like it since you're always writing in notebooks. We used our piggy banks and dad made up the difference." The boys all talked at once while Wendy tried to make sense of her LATCH present showing up as a gift from the boys. She felt dizzy. She itched to open it, but waited.

"You are the best," Wendy threw her arms around all three boys. "It's absolutely perfect."

After a big Christmas breakfast, Wendy went to her room. She held her breath as she opened the lock on her new moon journal. Gently, she flipped through the pages. Nothing. She was disappointed and relieved. Then, she noticed some small writing on one of the pages. She flipped the book open to get a better look and two torn halves of a photo, a familiar photo of a young woman, fluttered out. Wendy stood there frozen. She was unaware that Joey had appeared in the doorway.

"Did that come out of your journal?" he asked.

Wendy nodded, at first unable to speak. "It must have gotten stuck in there by accident," she whispered hoarsely.

"It was meant for you," Joey said simply.

Wendy met his eyes. Despite the fact that he was only four, she knew that he was right.

That's when she remembered the writing in the journal. She flipped back to the words. "You wrote this, didn't you?" Although, Joey knew some of his letters, as far as she knew, he couldn't read or write.

"I saw those letters printed over and over in your notebook. I figured they were important to you. I remembered how they looked and practiced copying them," Joey explained proudly. "They're L, A, T, C, H, right?" he asked.

"That's right."

"What do they mean?" Joey pressed.

Wendy wondered what she should say. "It's a club. I'll tell you about it when you're older."

Joey nodded, satisfied, as if he understood much more than the words she had spoken. "You'll tell me about it, when it's time for me . . . ," he added quietly.

Wendy had always known that Joey was special, that he instinctively sensed things which the other boys would never understand. But it had never occurred to her that he might be meant for LATCH. Now it seemed like the most natural thing in the world. "Yes," she agreed.

Chapter Thirty

The moonstone ring's charm seemed to hold all through Christmas vacation. The boys were happy, playing with their new toys, sleeping late. LATCH seemed to be on vacation, too. It was a relief not to encounter Phillip. The only thing Wendy really missed was talking to April.

And then it was New Year's Eve. Ralph and Liz had gone out, leaving Wendy with the boys. She didn't mind; it had been a peaceful evening. The boys had fallen asleep watching a movie. Wendy wanted to stay up till midnight, but she didn't know if she could stay awake herself.

Bong, bong, bong . . . On TV, the ball was about to drop at Times Square when Wendy arrived at the top of the world. Everywhere she looked she could see the lights of Manhattan. That's when she realized that she was standing on the eighty-sixth floor observation deck of the Empire State Building.

"Happy New Year!" April shouted to be heard over

the howling wind. "Isn't this a great place to celebrate the New Year? I can't wait until it's midnight."

For a second, Wendy forgot how time worked at LATCH. "Isn't it already midnight?" she asked. Then she remembered that it was really 4:00 A.M. The ball wouldn't be dropping for four hours.

"I'm so glad to see you." Wendy hugged April. "I've been wanting to talk to you."

"Oh, me too." April spotted Phillip staring at them, grabbed Wendy's hand and dragged her over to a more private corner. "The weirdest thing happened to me. When I opened my Christmas present from my aunt, it was a diary with a pearl moon on a midnight blue velvet background. Just like the journal we got at the LATCH holiday party."

Wendy bit her lip in excitement. "That's amazing. The boys found mine at the store. It was the only one. They said they knew it was right for me."

April shrugged her shoulders. "As I've said from the beginning, we can't pretend to understand this LATCH stuff."

Wendy took a deep breath, about to burst. "There's more. I never had a chance to tell you at the LATCH party, but my journal came with a small photo of a girl stuck in the pages."

"You're kidding!"

"I didn't even notice it at first. Phillip grabbed the journal from me, because he was suspicious of the way Petavius had chosen my gift. That's when the picture fell out. When I tried to take it back, it ripped in half. He thinks it's a photo of Serena, the girl that Petavius told me about at the Blue Moon Ball."

April shook her head.

"It gets more incredible," continued Wendy. "The

diary that the boys gave me had the exact same photo in it, torn in half the same way."

April looked like she had seen a ghost. "We'll just have to find out who she is . . ."

And then, Wendy and April almost screamed as Hercules' head appeared over the outside edge of the observation deck right in front of them, over one thousand feet above street level. That's when they noticed the mountaineering gear attached to the wall.

"Happy New Year!" he called out heartily. Wendy could tell that Hercules had never been happier than he was balancing on the railing with nothing between him and the street eighty-six stories below.

"Even though it's New Year's Eve, this is a regular R and R class. First we work, then we party," Hercules called out. "Everyone warm up on the steps, down and up fifty flights."

Hercules clapped his hands and the whole class was off. Of course, running down was easy. Now that Wendy was in better shape, it was really fun to move. The way back up was a different story. Everyone slowed down, but Wendy's legs didn't hurt at all. She seemed to sail up the stairs. Wendy couldn't believe it when she was the first one to arrive back on the observation deck.

Hercules' eyes widened when he saw her. "Hey, congratulations. You've come a long way from the summer."

April arrived second. "Boy, that double R and R has worked wonders for you."

Wendy was smiling and blushing at these compliments as Phillip arrived on the deck, clearly displeased that he had not made it up first. He was obviously not at all happy about having his athletic supremacy challenged, especially by Wendy. He was about to say something nasty to her, when Hercules announced that they were going to play Hercules Says, his version of Simon Says.

Spread out on the terrace, he had them imitate an elaborate set of exercises that he invented from every form of movement that he knew. They did handstands and splits. They juggled and balanced in peculiar yoga postures. They kick-boxed and fenced. Soon they were all laughing. One by one, they were eliminated from the game.

Eventually, only Nick, Phillip and Wendy were left. The class cheered them on. Hercules eyed the three of them and decided on his next challenge. "Hercules says, do this." He executed a complicated fencing thrust.

Wendy knew that she could do it. She knew that Hercules knew that she could do it. She sensed that Phillip was a keg of dynamite that was about to blow. Purposely, she flubbed the move.

Hercules stared at her in disbelief. "Wendy's out."

"Why did you miss?" April hissed.

"Because I'm feeling too good to set Phillip off tonight," Wendy whispered. "Let him win the silly game."

But Wendy did not get her wish. Phillip botched the next karate kick and Nick won the game. Phillip looked like a storm cloud. He never could handle losing.

Wendy tried to avoid him as she helped herself to some punch. In honor of New Year's Eve, they were having Yin Yang Punch. Hercules explained that the Chinese believed that there were balancing powers from the sun, Yang, and the moon, Yin, which composed most forces in life. He had chosen this drink to bring them balance in the New Year.

Wendy certainly hoped it would work as she scooped out the red and white swirling punch. The two parts didn't mix to form a pink liquid, but swirled separately like a pinwheel. The red part tasted like sun-ripened berries, the white like cream with a hint of chocolate and mint. It was delicious, unlike anything she had ever had.

"Now who would like to ring in the New Year by jumping over the side of the deck?" asked Hercules with a twinkle.

Without missing a beat, April shot forward. "I would." Wendy was surprised that Phillip didn't volunteer first. He prided himself on being the class daredevil. But Phillip was still sullen and distracted.

Hercules proceeded to hook April into an elaborate harness on a bungee cord. Wendy was really beginning to feel dizzy at the very idea. "I'm sorry, I can't look," she explained as she headed for the other side of the deck. She didn't hear Phillip follow her.

"What is your connection to Serena?" Phillip's voice cut through the howling wind. She whipped around. He was right in front of her, trapping her against the railing.

Wendy took a deep breath to stay calm. "Phillip, we've been over this and over this. I have no idea who Serena was. As you've pointed out many times, I'm a foster child. I have absolutely no family, no connections at all."

"Then why was that picture in your journal? Stop lying to me." Phillip was inches from Wendy, almost pushing her over the railing.

"Even if there was some connection, whatever happened between your father and Serena is ancient history. It's time to drop it," Wendy responded furiously.

"It is not ancient history. It is unfinished business, and I will never drop it," Phillip responded menacingly.

"Wendy?" April's voice was filled with alarm as she rounded the corner of the deck.

Instantly, Phillip stepped back. "How was the jump, April?" he asked charmingly, changing gears in an instant.

"That won't work on me, Huntie," April snapped as she moved away with Wendy. "What was that all about?" April asked.

"Phillip is convinced that I have some connection to Serena. Apparently, she was involved in the accident that injured his father at LATCH."

"For a second, I thought he was going to push you over." April was upset.

"I think he's just trying to frighten me. He's too scared of getting kicked out of LATCH to really hurt me. All of his family's hopes are pinned on him succeeding at LATCH and fulfilling their political dreams," Wendy said bravely.

"You've got to talk to Petavius," insisted April.

Wendy knew that April was right, but it was going to take some courage to find the right moment.

From high on the Empire State Building they could hear a roar as lights flickered several blocks away.

"I think the ball is dropping," April said. "Happy New Y. . . ."

Bong, bong, bong. Before April could finish, Wendy was back in her bed. More than anything, she wanted it to be a Happy New Year. But she couldn't help feeling that her latest confrontation with Phillip foreshadowed more trouble.

Chapter Thirty-one

Wendy used her new journal to assess her progress at LATCH. New Year's Eve had been an eye-opener for her. She loved remembering Hercules' face when she had arrived on the deck first. Pedro never stopped teasing her about how she was the star in Cloud Counting. She was the first one to successfully hypnotize someone. She had made Pedro act like an elephant. Eclipse, her transformation activity, was very technical. She was learning how to observe and imitate, but Wendy still had trouble with certain exercises that involved becoming someone very confident or arrogant. And then there was Illumination, where Diana was working on their belief in themselves. For some reason, Wendy felt she was going backwards in Illumination. She was more afraid to try things than she had been at the beginning.

"Wendy, is something bothering you?" Diana asked gently at the end of one of their sessions.

Diana's voice was so encouraging that Wendy felt herself opening up. She had been trying to get up the courage to speak to Petavius about Serena, but she couldn't make herself ask. Wendy decided that this was the moment.

"Years ago, did you know someone at LATCH named Serena?" Wendy asked.

Diana smiled. "I've heard of her, of course. Serena made quite a name for herself. She set all the records in concentration activities. Why do you ask?"

"What did Serena do to Phillip's father? Phillip told me that his father was seriously hurt because of Serena. . . ."

Diana frowned. "I wasn't around at the time, but I do believe that there was some incident during their Galileo Quest that ended badly."

"Galileo Quest?" Wendy repeated.

"Oh, that's right. You haven't been on a quest yet, have you? Sometimes I forget that you're only a New Mooner. Each LATCH phase ends with a Galileo Quest, an adventure in which you use what you've learned in the preceding year to solve the quest."

"So we all take the Galileo Quest at the end of the year, like an exam?" Wendy was already worried.

Diana laughed musically. "It's not a test. It's more like a wonderful game designed especially for you. The quest is named for Galileo, who was the first scientist to study the moon through a telescope and draw maps of it. You'll find you'll really look forward to the Galileo Quests. You learn so much about yourself."

Wendy was unnerved to hear Diana confirm that Phillip's father had been hurt at LATCH and that somehow Serena was connected. Although they did risky things sometimes, she had always felt that the magic of LATCH protected them from getting injured. Apparently that wasn't true.

* * *

Wendy knew that she had to talk to Petavius now more than ever, but there never seemed to be an opportunity. At the end of an Eclipse session, when she would finally work up the courage to approach him, she would find herself back in her bed. She didn't know how to call or write to him. She couldn't figure out how she was ever going to get him alone.

At her next session, Wendy sought him out right at the beginning. "I need to talk to you, Petavius."

Petavius looked up distractedly. "Oh, Wendy. How are you, my dear?"

"Could I talk to you at the end? It's important," Wendy repeated.

Petavius smiled benevolently. "Of course, my dear."

Wendy pressed on, "I've tried to stay before, but I've always been whisked back home."

"I'll make sure that doesn't happen tonight," Petavius assured her.

Wendy did very badly with her transformation exercises that night. She was distracted about her talk with Petavius. She hoped he would remember to stop her from traveling home. The clock was just striking midnight as she approached him. Before she could get to him, she sensed that her body was getting lighter with the rush of wind surrounding her. "Pet!" she called out in a panic.

He looked up, startled, and only then seemed to remember their appointment. Her body jerked as if it had suddenly gotten heavier and the sound of the wind disappeared. Petavius looked sheepish. "Sorry, I tend to be a bit absentminded."

Petavius finally gave her all his considerable focus. "What is it, my dear? What is bothering you?"

Petavius's clear gray eyes were staring right into hers. "Things are very confusing for me. . . ." Wendy's voice trailed off.

"Confusing in what way?" Petavius looked truly concerned.

"It all started at the Blue Moon Ball, when you told me about Serena, when I told Phillip about her by accident."

Petavius' brow creased. "That was an unfortunate turn of events."

Wendy burst out, "Phillip believes that Serena destroyed his father's life and that I'm connected to her somehow."

In a split second, a thousand different looks passed over Petavius's face, and then it returned to its normal inscrutable self. "It's true," he answered slowly. "Phillip's father was hurt during his Galileo Quest. He and Serena were in the same phase together. But in no way was Serena responsible."

"But he thinks she was," Wendy interrupted.

"I know. The Huntington family is very gifted, but they always try to blame someone else for their own mistakes. I will talk to Phillip," Petavius said firmly.

This was just what Wendy had been dreading. "I wish you wouldn't. He already seems to hate me."

Petavius looked like he might explode. "I have been handling Huntingtons for three generations. Phillip has no reason to hate you. There is no connection between you and Serena."

Wendy had her answer. "What about the photo in my holiday moon journal?"

"What photo?" Pet snapped.

Wendy could see that Petavius genuinely didn't know what she was talking about. "There was a photo of a beautiful dark-haired girl tucked in my journal."

"I don't know how it got there. All the New Moon gifts were exactly the same."

"But you purposely put back the first gift you selected for me and handed me another one," Wendy reminded him.

"I don't remember doing that. But most likely, I was making sure that I gave you the right gift for your phase." Petavius was growing impatient.

"So you didn't intend to give me that photo?" Wendy pressed him.

"I had no idea it was there." Petavius was definite.

Wendy was silent. She had nothing more to ask.

Petavius' voice grew gentle. "Let me remind you, Wendy, that unlike many young people at LATCH, you have accomplished everything in life on your own. You should feel very proud of yourself."

Wendy had barely digested this compliment when the wind rushed by her ears. Petavius had ended their interview.

Wendy awoke in the middle of the night. She had been dreaming of the girl with the dark hair. But every time Wendy got close to her she disappeared around the corner. Wendy got her moon journal out of its hiding place and flipped to the back pages. There was the ripped photo. How had it come to be there?

Chapter Thirty-two

Talking to Petavius helped. She kept remembering his words, that she had accomplished everything on her own. That was exactly what she had vowed to do on her birthday. It didn't matter why her parents had left her. It didn't matter about Serena. She was tired of thinking about all the mysteries of her life. Once and for all, she decided to focus on the present and make the most of it.

It didn't hurt that Phillip seemed to have backed off. Wendy had been worried that Phillip would lash out at her if Petavius spoke to him. But, if anything, Phillip seemed to be staying out of her way. Maybe everything was going to be okay.

The big event at school was the upcoming school play. Hannah never stopped talking about the auditions. They were doing *Pippi Longstocking* and Hannah was determined to get the part of Pippi.

"I've memorized all the lines already," Hannah told Wendy proudly.

Wendy was worried for her friend. She had never

seen Hannah perform, although she figured Hannah was pretty good because she took acting classes after school. However, Wendy was all too aware that getting cast depended on school politics and who your friends were. Hannah was still very much on the social fringe of the school, just like Wendy.

"Look, Hannah, I don't think you should set your heart on Pippi," Wendy cautioned her friend.

"Why? Are you going for Pippi, too? I knew it. You'd be perfect," Hannah said grudgingly.

Wendy burst out laughing. "Me! You've got to be kidding. I'll be lucky if I get the part of the school teacher. I'm so tall and dumpy, I always get cast as an adult."

Now, it was Hannah's turn to burst out laughing. "Have you looked in a mirror lately? You may be a little tall, but there's nothing dumpy about you. You're in great shape."

Wendy was taken aback. She had noticed that her clothes were getting pretty loose. "That's nice of you to say, but I'm telling you, if I get a part it will be something no one else wants. I wouldn't even think of reading for Pippi."

Hannah looked puzzled. "Well, if you're sure, maybe you'll practice some scenes with me?"

"Sure," Wendy agreed.

For days, Hannah and Wendy stole time to practice. Wendy usually read the parts of Tommy or Annika, Pippi's friends. They loved rehearsing and often ended up doubled over with laughter.

Finally, the big day of the auditions came. Wendy got to the sign-up board right after school. She was sure that Hannah would be there any minute.

Angela and all the popular girls came up to the board. Wendy tried to become invisible.

It didn't work.

"Hilton, are you trying out for Pippi?" Angela asked aggressively.

Wendy was baffled for the second time. "Oh, no."

The group burst out giggling and Angela turned away, a satisfied smile on her lips.

Mrs. Dulcimer, the director, handed out scenes and then disappeared into the theater. Wendy couldn't imagine what was keeping Hannah when she heard a commotion. Parading down the hall was a girl dressed in high mismatched socks and a patched dress. Her hair was a shocking carrot red in two peculiar braids. It was Hannah!

"What did you do?" stammered Wendy.

"These people are so unimaginative. Since I have dark hair, I thought I better help them picture me as Pippi. I just colored it in the girls' room. That's why I'm late," Hannah said proudly.

"Everyone's laughing at you," Wendy whispered, embarrassed.

"The theater is all about taking risks. And Pippi is the biggest risk taker of them all. She wouldn't care if people laughed at her," Hannah responded breezily.

Wendy admired her friend's boldness. Diana would approve. Wendy hoped that it wouldn't backfire on Hannah.

Just then, the doors opened. "Wendy and Hannah," Mrs. Dulcimer called out, looking down at her sheet. "Oh my," she said when she noticed Hannah's outfit. "Can I assume that you want to read for Pippi?"

"Yes, please," Hannah smiled confidently. "Can Wendy read Annika with me?"

Mrs. Dulcimer nodded. "I don't see why not."

"Just do it like we practiced," whispered Hannah before they began. "Don't stop, whatever I do."

Wendy began her first line. She was stiff and nervous. Then she looked up. Hannah was skipping around, walking on her hands, making faces into an imaginary mirror, being Pippi. Wendy couldn't help laughing, just like Annika would have when she met this outrageous girl. Somehow, Wendy managed to continue the scene, but Hannah never stopped surprising her. Wendy found herself infected by Pippi's sense of fun. By the end of the scene, Wendy was also trying to do a handstand.

Wendy looked for her next line. But the scene was over. Only then did Wendy return to reality. She looked at Mrs. Dulcimer, who was furiously scribbling notes. "Thank you, girls." She seemed to be dismissing them.

"But I have to read my scene, the teacher's scene," Wendy sputtered.

"That's not necessary. You may go. I have a lot of students to see today," Mrs. Dulcimer said firmly. "Angela and Zachary," she called.

Angela glared at Hannah as they crossed paths in the aisle. Wendy could hear Angela complaining, "I don't think that's fair. We didn't know we were supposed to dress up. . . ."

Mrs. Dulcimer had promised to post the casting the next morning. Wendy got there early and forced herself to walk up to the board. She hoped that Hannah wouldn't be too disappointed. Wendy knew that there was no chance they would get leads. The director always had the top candidates read several times. They had only been allowed to read once.

Wendy raised her eyes. It couldn't be right!

And then, someone was shrieking and jumping on her back. "We did it! We did it!" Hannah almost knocked Wendy over. There it was.

PIPPI: HANNAH GREEN
ANNIKA: WENDY HILTON

"I told you we were the best!" Hannah crowed just as Angela and her pals rounded the corner.

Angela flipped her hair and glanced at the board as if she couldn't care less. "The best? Looks like a sympathy vote to me. After that hair stunt, Mrs. Dulcimer must have figured you were desperate," Angela said snidely. Her group giggled on cue and then flounced off.

Hannah was not deflated. "She's just jealous. Wait till she deals with us in the classroom scenes."

And that's when Wendy finally noticed that Angela, the most popular girl in their class, was cast as the schoolteacher.

Chapter Thirty-three

Wendy tossed and turned that night. What had Hannah gotten her into? She was thrilled about getting the part, but convinced that she wouldn't be good enough. And since she had one of the leads, the rehearsal schedule was a killer. She knew that some of the rehearsals would run late, and that would make tending to her responsibilities with the boys more difficult. If she backed out, she was afraid that Hannah would never forgive her.

Bong, bong, bong, bong . . .

It was such a relief to escape from her real life tonight. Her body felt light. She seemed to float into the dark and tranquil space. Just what she needed. The stark beauty of the Cloisters. Cloud Counting. Already, she could feel her shoulders relaxing.

"Hey, buddy," came a smiling voice.

"Pedro, I'm so glad to see you. What a day," Wendy sighed.

"What's up?" asked Pedro, and Wendy told him everything.

"The rehearsals are no problem," smiled Pedro. "I live nearby. If you get stuck, I'll pick the boys up."

Wendy couldn't believe Pedro's generosity. "You'd do that? Don't you have a job after school?"

"Stop focusing on obstacles. Haven't you learned anything from Cloud Counting? Persephone is always telling us to clear the path, to block doubts from filtering into our thinking. So stop it. If I said I can do it, you can count on me."

It finally sank in. Wendy's face lit up like a Christmas tree. "You're the best," she said, hugging Pedro.

"Can we begin?" Persephone's soft voice cut through the room.

Back at the Cloisters for the first time since the fall, Persephone had set up a number of candles again. They started working in groups. After they were warmed up, Persephone had them work individually. Lots of the kids took a long time concentrating to get an individual wick to flicker to life.

Eventually, it was Wendy's turn. For some reason, the minute she concentrated, the candles leapt into flame. Persephone started to call out different candles, faster. Wendy just had to glance at the right candle and it was burning. She closed her eyes and pictured them in her head. She could still ignite them. Everyone was quiet as Wendy worked.

Instead of calling out a single candle, Persephone challenged Wendy. "The left candelabra." Without missing a beat, all seven candles were suddenly burning. Persephone called out the right candelabra. Wendy, totally in a zone, smiled. In sequence, the candles burst into flame from left to right. And then an extraordinary thing happened. The candelabra seemed to fill with so much energy that it actually moved ten inches to the right, as if it were alive.

There was a gasp, and the Half Mooners started clapping.

Persephone held up her hand to quiet them. "That was an example of telekinesis, which is usually covered in the fifth phase, the Full Moon phase. Very impressive, Miss Hilton. Your energy is very focused tonight."

Wendy felt self-conscious as everyone came up to congratulate her.

"That was awesome," Helena said. "How did you do it?"

"I don't know," Wendy answered truthfully. "But something that Pedro said earlier about clearing the path really made sense. I just didn't feel any obstacles tonight. Then it was easy."

"I said what Persephone has said a hundred times before," Pedro insisted.

"Well, however you said it, it hit home," Wendy said modestly. "Thanks."

"Now, if I could only convince myself," Pedro grinned. "Let me know about the rehearsals," he added.

"I just have to clear it with Liz," Wendy said.

"I'll stop by and introduce myself," Pedro volunteered.

"That's a good idea," Wendy said. Then she thought of something. "But tell her that we met through your cousins who live in our building."

Pedro winked. "Got it. I'm not sure she'd understand about LATCH."

Wendy grinned. "I don't understand about LATCH."

Pedro looked untroubled. "Join the party. I told you, none of us do."

Chapter Thirty-four

That night at Cloud Counting was a turning point for Wendy. Even though she was very nervous at her first rehearsal, convinced that Mrs. Dulcimer would think that she made a mistake, once she was with Hannah they had so much fun that little by little Wendy began to let go of her doubts.

Zachary was playing Tommy, Annika's brother. At first, Zachary had a hard time blending into the chemistry that Hannah and Wendy had already developed with each other. But their zany mood was infectious, and soon he was having as much fun as they were.

This made Angela more jealous than ever. Not only had Hannah and Wendy stolen the parts that she considered rightfully hers, but now Zachary, one of the coolest boys in school, was going over to their side.

The day came when they had to rehearse their first scene with Angela as the schoolteacher. Angela was nasty and tried to give them a hard time. But Wendy

and Hannah ignored her and were relentlessly play-
ful. By the end of the scene, a frustrated Angela realized that she could not get to them. She finally had
to give in and join the fun.

Rehearsals got more and more frantic as they got
closer to the first performance. Hannah had trouble
walking in her oversized shoes without tripping.
Everyone was always laughing so hard at Pippi's
madcap behavior that they forgot their lines. The
school scene had so many kids in it that it was total
chaos. Mrs. Dulcimer's normally sweet temperament
was getting frayed.

Wendy knew that there was no way she was going
to get out on time for her final two rehearsals. She
talked to Pedro and Helena at Cloud Counting.

"I was afraid that you were never going to take me
up on my offer," Pedro said. "I'll stop by your rehearsal to get the keys and then I'll pick up the
boys."

Wendy's eyes shone. She was so lucky to have Pedro as her buddy. LATCH had given her Pedro and
April. And if she thought about it, LATCH had given
her the confidence to get to know Hannah, too.

Everyone was terribly nervous on Wednesday at the
technical rehearsal. This was the first time that they
were working with the lights, the curtain and the
finished sets. It was very hard for the actors, because
they had to keep stopping and starting scenes for
the backstage crew.

Mrs. Dulcimer kept gnawing on her lip, expecting
the worst. But, amazingly, everything seemed to
work out pretty well. It wasn't the dress rehearsal, so

they weren't wearing their costumes, except for Hannah, who was still trying to get used to her shoes. But today Hannah seemed to have gotten the hang of them. She didn't stumble once. Wendy found that she was so comfortable being Annika that she wasn't even nervous.

They were well into the second act when Pedro found her in the darkened auditorium. "How's it going?" he whispered.

Wendy pulled out her keys. "Pretty well. I don't think I'll be too late."

Pedro could tell she couldn't talk. "See you later."

Angela came up to Wendy after Pedro had left. "Who was that?"

Wendy stiffened, waiting for one of Angela's biting comments. "My friend, Pedro."

"He's cute," Angela said admiringly.

"Well, I don't know whether to be elated or terrified," announced Mrs. Dulcimer, "but, that was one of the smoothest technical rehearsals in the history of the theater."

"That's not good," whispered Hannah. "People in the theater are superstitious. They believe that bad tech and dress rehearsals are good luck."

"I'm so proud of all of you. We'll be back for dress rehearsal at 3:30 sharp tomorrow," Mrs. Dulcimer finished.

Hannah stood up and let out an enormous sneeze.

"Are you okay?" Wendy asked anxiously.

"Pippi is always better than okay," Hannah winked in her Pippi way. "It's just the smell of the fresh paint on the sets. Allergies."

* * *

Hannah's allergies were worse the next day. She kept forgetting her lines and tripping. She never stopped sneezing.

"Are you sure those are allergies?" asked Wendy, concerned. "You seem sick."

"Pippi is never sick," Hannah replied defiantly. "Anyhow, I think my red nose matches my red hair perfectly. It's a brilliant touch."

Wendy couldn't help thinking that Hannah's eyes were unnaturally shiny. The boys' eyes looked like that when they had a fever.

Mrs. Dulcimer came up to them at that moment. "I've called your mother, Hannah. She's coming to take you home. I'm excusing you from the rest of rehearsal."

Hannah looked like she was going to burst into tears. "But you can't finish rehearsal without Pippi!"

"We'll have no show without Pippi. It's more important for you to go home and get better for tomorrow," Mrs. Dulcimer stated firmly.

Rehearsal, which had been going badly with Hannah, was a disaster after she left. Wendy tried to help with Hannah's lines, but they weren't even finished with Act One when Pedro arrived.

"Good news," Wendy whispered. "Hannah is sick and everything is going wrong."

Pedro grinned at Wendy's black humor. "Congratulations. I guess you'll be late then."

"You're a good guesser," responded Wendy.

At 8:00 P.M. Mrs. Dulcimer finally ended the rehearsal even though they hadn't finished the final scene of the birthday party.

She tried to smile through her strained white lips. "Well, we were worried about how well everything went yesterday. Now, we don't have to worry anymore. Go home. Forget about the play and rest. See you tomorrow night."

Angela raised her hand. "What if Hannah can't go on tomorrow?"

Mrs. Dulcimer looked as if she'd like to wring Angela's neck. "That is why Hannah went home early, to get well. She'll be fine tomorrow."

Wendy dragged herself home. Pedro was waiting for her. "Look, I really hate to mention this to you right now. But something weird happened when I picked up the boys."

The knot in Wendy's stomach clenched tighter. "What?"

"When I arrived, a black limo was in front of the day care center. It seemed really out of place. When I walked in, the woman at the desk got upset. She told me that a man in the limo had come to pick up the boys. Apparently, he had convinced her that I had sent him. He knew my name and everything. I rushed out to the limo in time and got the boys. Unfortunately, I hardly saw the driver before he took off, but I noticed an H on his uniform cap."

Wendy felt sick. "You think the H was for Huntington? That Phillip was up to something?" she whispered.

"Who else could it be?" Pedro asked.

"Why would he do that?" Wendy was shaken.

"I think he wants to scare you. You threaten him," Pedro said seriously. "Helena told me that he's always talking about you. He's asked her a thousand questions about the candelabra moving at Cloud Counting. I think that's how he knew about me picking up the boys from day care . . . from Helena."

Even though she had hardly interacted with Phillip since she had talked to Petavius, Wendy had known deep down that Phillip had not given up. And now, he was trying to get at her through the boys. All her concerns about Hannah and the play faded in comparison.

Pedro could see how upset Wendy was. "Nothing bad happened. The day care center knows that they should never release the boys again to anyone who's not on the list."

Wendy nodded numbly. "I want to go see the boys. . . ."

Somehow, Wendy managed to kiss the boys goodnight and get herself to bed. She felt ill at the thought of what might have happened. Where would Phillip stop?

Chapter Thirty-five

When the phone rang at 6:30 A.M., Wendy had been awake for a long time. She raced to the phone, sensing that it was for her. All she heard was a horrible scratching sound followed by a fit of coughing.

"Wendy?" Wendy recognized Hannah's mother. "That was Hannah. She wanted to tell you herself, but she's lost her voice completely. I've called Mrs. Dulcimer. Barring some miracle, Hannah is not going to be able to perform tonight."

In a way, it was a relief that Hannah was sick. Wendy felt so drained that she would have been terrible tonight. Now that the performance would be canceled, she thought about calling in sick for school. But she had to drop off the boys, so she figured she might as well go.

She was surprised to see Mrs. Dulcimer hovering by the door of her homeroom.

"You're late. I've been waiting for you. Come with me," Mrs. Dulcimer snapped. "I've cleared you from all your classes today." Mrs. Dulcimer talked as she raced in the direction of the auditorium.

"Where are we going?" Wendy asked, trying to keep up.

"I don't want to tell anyone else yet, but I've got an idea how we can have a performance tonight." Mrs. Dulcimer gave her a secret smile. "I need your help."

Wendy was very curious about Mrs. Dulcimer's plan. She prayed it wasn't to give the part to snotty Angela.

On the stage, Mrs. Dulcimer asked Wendy to show her where Pippi stood on stage as they ran through several scenes. "Thank you. My notes were incomplete. Angela and Zachary will be here any minute."

Wendy's heart sank. Angela was taking over. How in the world could Wendy play her scenes with Angela as Pippi? It would be awful, a betrayal.

Mrs. Dulcimer fished in her tote bag. "I have a present for you, Wendy."

Wendy was very confused as Mrs. Dulcimer handed her a small box: "Fire Engine Red: Hair Rinse #5." Wendy stared at Mrs. Dulcimer blankly. Nothing made sense.

Mrs. Dulcimer spoke very gently, as if she were dealing with a skittish animal. "I bought this last night, Wendy. As soon as Hannah left, I realized that you knew all of Pippi's lines cold. I knew you could do the part."

"Oh no. I can't. I really can't!" Wendy panicked.

Mrs. Dulcimer's face hardened. "We've sold two hundred tickets for tonight. The show must go on. I know you can do it."

"But I won't be the same as Hannah," Wendy protested.

"Maybe not. But I think you would be the best one to take over," Mrs. Dulcimer said firmly.

What did that mean? Would Mrs. Dulcimer let Angela go on if she wouldn't? That would be horrible. Wendy couldn't deny that she knew the part. If she could just clear the obstacles in her brain . . .

"All right." Wendy took a deep breath. "I'll try."

Angela's face fell when she walked into the theater and spotted Wendy's still wet, red hair. She immediately cornered Mrs. Dulcimer for a private conference.

"You look good as a redhead," Zachary said as he came up to Wendy. "Angela was positive that she was going to take over Pippi. Thank goodness you're doing it."

Wendy was touched by his vote of confidence.

Angela was a little red in the face when she emerged from her talk with Mrs. Dulcimer. "I'm so excited that I'm going to play Annika," she chirped brightly. "Good thing I'm a quick study."

"I hope so," Mrs. Dulcimer said dryly.

They ran through the whole play before lunch. Angela seemed to be doing everything she could to throw Wendy off. Wendy fell down the porch steps and skinned her knees the first time she tried the Pippi shoes. Zachary tried to hold things together.

After a lunch break, they crammed in a combined tech/dress rehearsal. True to her word, Angela seemed to have mastered her lines over lunch. She was full of energy and fun. On the contrary, Wendy felt like a piece of wood. She wasn't lively and zany like Hannah. Maybe it would have been better for Angela to play Pippi.

Mrs. Dulcimer took Wendy aside after Act One.

"You know all the lines perfectly, Wendy. But Pippi is different from Annika. She is the leader, not the follower. We need to see a little more zip. Like Hannah."

Wendy thought about Petavius and Eclipse. She thought about becoming Cleopatra at the Blue Moon Ball. She had transformed herself before. With the costume, hair and freckles, she looked just like Hannah. She could be Hannah.

When they started the second act Wendy focused her energy on acting like Hannah. She bounded around doing tricks and making silly faces, imitating Hannah's performance perfectly. It felt a little forced to Wendy, but it was better than tripping over her own feet and giving a wooden performance.

When the birthday party ended, Mrs. Dulcimer ran up on stage and hugged all three of them. "I can't believe how hard you've worked. Go home and rest. It's going to be a great night."

Mrs. Dulcimer came up to Wendy as she was leaving. "No one will ever know that you are an understudy. You are exactly like Hannah."

As Wendy was walking home, she wondered why she felt so empty.

Wendy called Pedro when she got home. "Hannah lost her voice. I'm playing Pippi tonight."

Pedro let out a whistle. "When it rains it pours. I'm coming over right now."

Wendy tried to rest, but thoughts of Pippi kept filling her head. When she thought about it, Pippi was really a lot like her. Her parents were gone. She had to do everything for herself. And, although she acted funny, it wasn't always fun to be alone.

Pedro arrived. "How are you doing?"

"You know, you were right about LATCH. I thought

there was no way I could play Pippi. But, when I believed I could and concentrated, I was able to."

"See, that's why it doesn't matter if LATCH is only a bunch of dreams or not. The effect is real. A year ago, you would never have been able to pull this off, would you?"

"Absolutely not. I didn't realize how much I've learned." Wendy hesitated. "But I keep thinking of Petavius. He always tells us to transform from the inside out. Instead, I feel like I've become Pippi on the outside only."

"When you're asked to take over the lead the day of the performance, all you're expected to do is get through it," Pedro said practically.

Wendy sighed. "Never in a million years did I think I'd ever be in this position. But now that I am, I want to make the most of it . . . if I don't die of stage fright. I want Pippi to be my Pippi."

Chapter Thirty-six

Just before the performance, Wendy was shaking in the wings when a smiling Angela came up to her. "Break a leg," she whispered, then giggled. "And you just might in those shoes," she added wickedly.

"Places," called Mrs. Dulcimer.

Wendy took the stuffed monkey, Mr. Nillson, on her arm and headed for her opening mark on stage. It was pitch dark. With all her might, she concentrated on becoming Pippi.

"Due to illness, the part of Pippi Longstocking is being played by Wendy Hilton." Mrs. Dulcimer's announcement echoed through the auditorium.

Wendy's focus was shattered by the sound of her name. Her arm trembled so noticeably that Mr. Nillson seemed to bob up and down like a real monkey. "How in the world did we get into this, Mr. Nillson?" she whispered frantically.

The curtain rose and for a split second Wendy was blinded by the stage lights. The audience burst into applause when they saw Pippi. Wendy couldn't believe they were all looking at her. Then she realized they weren't watching Wendy, they were watching Pippi.

That seemed to activate her. She bounded up the steps to her new home, the Villa Villekula. She noticed that Mr. Nillson looked sad. "Don't worry, Mr. Nillson. We're going to have fun here. I'll make sure of it."

Those weren't the exact lines in the script, but they felt right.

Wendy felt herself becoming Pippi. She flew around like a mini tornado, unpacking her trunks, doing cartwheels and balancing on the railing.

This was Tommy and Annika's cue. Confidently, Angela made her entrance with Zachary. Then she caught a glimpse of the audience and something happened.

Annika had the first line. It was "Who are you?"

Pippi waited and waited. Wendy looked into Angela's eyes. They were unblinking, terrified, like a deer frozen in the headlights. Wendy took charge. "Hello, I'm Pippilotta Delicatessa Windowshade Machrelmint Ephraim's Daughter Longstocking."

By now, Zachary had figured out what was happening. Somehow, they got through the scene without Angela saying one line. Zachary led her through their blocking holding her hand.

The lights dipped to black, and Angela headed for the wings. "I can't do it," she whispered, tears streaming down her face.

Wendy didn't hesitate. She took Angela by the shoulders. "Yes, you can. You're not Angela, worried about making a fool of yourself as the most popular girl in the school. You're Annika. Just look at me on stage. Don't look at the audience. I promise you, we'll have a blast." And with that, Wendy firmly led Angela back out on stage.

The instant the lights came up, Pippi started calling out instructions to Tommy and Annika to play an elaborate game. She didn't give Angela time to think. Somehow, it worked. Eventually, Angela forgot her terror and got into the game.

That's how they got through the first act. When the curtain came down for the intermission, Mrs. Dulcimer came up to Wendy. "You were brilliant, keeping Angela from freezing up. Thank you."

"It's what Pippi would have done," Wendy explained simply.

Angela seemed to have gotten through the worst of her stage fright by the second act. The play zoomed along at a madcap pace. Before they realized it, it was the birthday scene. They ate cake and played games. Then Tommy and Annika's father came to take them home.

Pippi watched them leave as she sat on the porch rocking chair with Mrs. Nillson on her lap. The moon shone overhead. "Goodnight, Mr. Nillson," Pippi said, fondly scratching the monkey. She looked at the moon. "Goodnight, Momma. Goodnight, Papa . . . wherever you are." Pippi raised one of the pistols that they had found in the trunk in the attic and let off a shot. The sound reverberated through the theater. All alone again, she leaned back and closed her eyes. The curtain closed.

The audience was silent for a moment and then applause exploded in the auditorium. Mrs. Dulcimer was clapping and crying in the wings. The cast was gathering for their curtain calls. But Pippi was still resting in her rocking chair.

A figure slipped on stage and came up to Wendy. "You were wonderful," Hannah hissed, her voice a little better.

Wendy opened her eyes. And then it all came back to her. "Oh, Hannah, you're here. Was it okay?"

Hannah looked at her curiously. "You have no idea, do you? You were incredible. Your Pippi was really something special."

Wendy felt her face redden. "I couldn't be Pippi like you. I hope you don't mind."

"The only thing that I mind is that your Pippi was better than mine," Hannah confided honestly.

"Don't be silly. I didn't get nearly as many laughs as you would have," Wendy claimed.

"But your Pippi was more real. I never thought about what it must be like for her to be all alone."

"I couldn't help it," Wendy admitted softly.

"In any case, maybe we'll see which works better tomorrow, if Mrs. Dulcimer lets me have the part back," Hannah teased. "And I have the advantage of a better Annika, assuming you can change gears overnight. Now, you better take your curtain calls."

With Angela on one side and Zachary on the other, Wendy bowed. When she looked out on the sea of faces, it was almost too much for her. There was Pedro holding Eddie on his lap, surrounded by Ralphie, Joey and April. Wendy was so thrilled that they were all there. The audience wouldn't stop clapping. Suddenly, Angela and Zachary let go of her hands, and Wendy was taking a bow alone. The sound of the audience doubled. Wendy had never experienced anything like it in her life.

Finally, the curtain came down. Wendy tried to catch her breath. She had never felt so drained. She turned to go and discovered Angela waiting in the darkness a few feet from her.

Angela looked like a ghost. "I was pretty full of myself this morning. Well, let's face it, I'm pretty full of myself every day. I thought I should have been the one to take over Pippi. Was I wrong! You were awesome. What's more, you saved me. I doubt if I could have been as generous as you were. Thank you." Angela held out her hand. They shook solemnly.

Mrs. Dulcimer appeared and Angela slipped away.

"I'm sorry, Mrs. Dulcimer," Wendy mumbled. "I know I changed a few things. I hope it didn't screw things up too much."

Mrs. Dulcimer just shook her head and smiled. "Hannah was right to worry. You are extremely talented, Wendy. Your Pippi was such a mix of boldness and vulnerability. I think you have a real future in the theater."

Wendy couldn't believe her ears. "Thank you. That means everything to me."

The next day, Hannah's voice was much better. Wendy was happy that her friend could perform. Their chemistry as Pippi and Annika had never been better. Zachary was great, now that he didn't have to worry about covering for Angela. And Angela was delighted to go back to being the schoolteacher.

There wasn't the special hush after the curtain came down that Wendy had received, but the audience clapped just as enthusiastically.

Mrs. Dulcimer gathered the cast and crew on stage after the last curtain call. "Whew, what an experience. You all rose to the challenge magnificently. I think both of our Pippis deserve a memento of their performances. Hannah, I'd like to present you with the pirate pistol for your swashbuckling Pippi. And, Wendy, I think we all agree that you should have Mr. Nillson, whom you brought to life as Pippi's dearest friend."

Everyone applauded as Wendy studied the bedraggled stuffed monkey. He looked pretty fake right now, but last night she would have sworn that he was alive. He would always remind her of her big night.

Chapter Thirty-seven

Everyone at school knew Wendy's name now. She was no longer invisible. More importantly, it was clear to everyone that Angela had accepted Wendy as one of her friends. Like sheep, many of the other kids followed Angela's example.

Although everything was much better at school, Wendy was not sleeping any better at night. She couldn't figure out what to do about Phillip. She dreaded what he might try next and thought about talking to Petavius again. But she really had no proof. Moreover, she realized that if she managed to get Phillip kicked out of LATCH, he could become a more dangerous enemy.

She was pretty sure that he wouldn't do anything that might jeopardize his future at LATCH. But if he was no longer in LATCH, he would have nothing to lose. She hadn't been so afraid when it just involved her. She couldn't take any chances with the boys, though. So she decided not to say anything to Petavius.

She considered confronting Phillip herself. But if he knew that he was scaring her, he would feel his plan was working and try more. She decided to ignore him.

Playing Pippi had taught Wendy an important lesson. She finally believed that what she was learning at LATCH really worked. She just had to concentrate and focus on transforming herself into the best that she could be and not worry about other people.

So while all the New Moon kids were panicking about the Galileo Quest, Wendy had a very positive attitude. She chose to believe what Diana had said, that it was like a wonderful game. She assumed that she would rise to the occasion.

"Aren't you worried at all?" April asked incredulously. "They say the challenges are always in your weakest areas. In my case, I'm sure it will be a concentration task."

"Isn't that what makes a game really good? It wouldn't be any fun, if it wasn't hard," Wendy replied.

"What happened to the nervous Wendy Hilton, shaking at the Central Park Zoo? You are altogether too mellow since your big stage triumph. I'm not sure I like having our roles reversed," April complained.

"Why do they have to be reversed? You're the one who persuaded me to believe. Students have been surviving their Galileo Quests for years."

"Phillip's father didn't . . . ," April muttered.

"We both know that Phillip's father must have done something to create his own disaster. Just like Phillip always does. We are not like them," Wendy said firmly.

"I just wish we knew when the Quest was going to take place," fussed April.

"It'll probably be the night of a full moon," said

Wendy. "Those nights have the most magic. Remember the Statue of Liberty and the Blue Moon Ball?"

"You're probably right," April said.

Between LATCH and the end of the school year, Wendy was so busy that she completely forgot that her birthday was approaching. In fact, it was the last day of school when she realized that it was June 21. She might not have remembered at all if Hannah hadn't surprised her with a homemade card and a book on acting.

How different it had been for Wendy last year, when she had known that the only way she was going to celebrate was by herself. It was the night of her birthday that she had received her invitation to LATCH. Nothing had been the same since.

Wendy started to write in her New Moon journal, but she felt a little restless. After all, it was her birthday. Her fourteenth birthday. It seemed like a big step. She thought about the day when she would be grown up. When she wouldn't need to live with a foster family anymore. And, of course, she thought about her parents.

Suddenly Wendy knew how she wanted to celebrate this birthday. She looked out at the sky. Unlike last year, the moon was not full. In fact, Wendy could tell from her journal cover that it was a new moon and therefore not visible at all. Carefully, she got dressed in a nice outfit. She brushed her hair until it shone with gold highlights. For her final touch, she slipped on her moonstone ring.

Reverently, she got down her wicker basket with her most precious things: the Wendy's napkin, the Hilton towel, the program from *A Midsummer Night's Dream*, the broken dried rose, the tiny rolled-up invitation to LATCH, her white sister stone from April, one of the tiny folded notes from Shadow, two programs from *Pippi Longstocking*—one with her playing Annika, and the other with an insert announcing that she was playing Pippi, and finally the scruffy stuffed monkey, Mr. Nillson. One by one, she laid them on her bed.

Her eyes swept over all these meaningful objects. There were so many more than last year. Each one represented something very special. So much had happened in the last twelve months. It was overwhelming.

She fingered her silver necklace. Had all of the events of the last year come about because of LATCH? Or had she somehow made them happen? As she always did when she thought about LATCH, Wendy felt lightheaded. It was a mystery she would never understand.

She slipped her sister rock into her pocket. She placed everything else in her basket for her trip up the fire escape.

She flinched. What was that? Her head snapped up and there was a gleaming white grin in the shadows outside of her window. Pedro!

It was too early for LATCH. What was he doing here? He beckoned her to follow him. Forgetting her basket, she followed him up to the roof. She could hear the wind whispering around the chimney.

"Surprise!"

It wasn't the wind that had been whispering. From behind the chimney, April, Helena and Nick jumped out holding a birthday cake in the shape of a crescent moon.

Wendy's heart flipped. Her first surprise party ever.

"Make a wish," insisted April.

That was hard. So many good things had already

happened to her. But, there was one thing . . . Wendy blew the candles out.

They sat on a blanket and cut the cake. April pulled a stack of presents out from behind the chimney. Wendy's eyes widened. Only in her imagination had she ever had a party like this.

Her hands shaking, she opened a small package from Nick. It was a Statue of Liberty key chain.

"That's the first time I really got to know you. I'm sorry that I never got to punch Phillip for you that night, though," Nick said regretfully. "He's such a jerk."

Wendy couldn't believe Helena's gift. It was a very fancy makeup kit in an elegant leather case. Wendy was troubled that it was so expensive.

"Don't worry, I got it for free on a modeling job. I think it will be useful for your self-projection project next year," Helena added, almost reading her mind.

Pedro gave her an old copy of *Pippi Longstocking*. Inside was a photo he had taken of her the night she had played Pippi.

"Oh, thank you, Pedro. I can look at this to prove that it really happened," Wendy said.

"Maybe, that's what we should all do at LATCH. Bring a camera," Nick kidded.

Wendy saved April's gift for last. It was an art book from the Metropolitan Museum with *their* paintings marked. Wendy flipped it open to *The First Steps* by Van Gogh. She was silent as she remembered the overwhelming feelings of the night they'd entered the different works of art.

Wendy looked around at her friends. "Thank you so much," she said, tears filling her eyes. "This has been the best birthday I've ever had."

Wendy moved over to the railing to collect herself. Helena followed her. "I've been wanting to talk to you. I know from Pedro that I've inadvertently told Phillip information that I shouldn't have. I've always known that he was competitive and egotistical, but I never believed he would do anything really bad. Unfortunately, I'm not sure I was right. I haven't spoken to him for weeks. I wouldn't trust him if I were you."

Wendy felt sick. "Since the limo incident, nothing has happened."

"I know. That's what worries me. He's been too quiet and he may be planning something. Phillip and his father are convinced that you are going to ruin Phillip's chance for success at LATCH," Helena said.

"I wish I knew why that was," Wendy said, suddenly exhausted.

"Phillip can't stand anyone being better than him. That's why he's always been fine with me, because I was the black sheep cousin. No threat."

Wendy was baffled. How could anyone consider this spectacular girl a black sheep? "Well, thank you. I'll be careful."

Helena hesitated, looking grim, then spoke. "I have only recently learned how ruthless some of my family members are. The pattern seems to have started with my grandfather. Huntingtons will stop at nothing. I am ashamed of that."

Wendy could hardly pull herself out of her anxious thoughts when April came up to her. "Thank you for the wonderful party. I know you were behind it."

April grinned. "You didn't think I'd forget, did you?"

Bong, bong, bong, bong . . .

Wendy was about to answer, when that distinctive rush of noise filled her ears. They had lost track of time. It was midnight.

Chapter Thirty-eight

Bong, bong, bong . . . Suddenly, the sound of flapping wings mingled with the bells. Wendy felt like she was being lifted by the back of her shirt. One of the enormous stone eagles was flying her over Central Park. Wendy wondered what activity this was going to be.

She remembered that April had talked to her eagle. "Who are you? Where are we going?" Wendy shouted.

The bird just looked at her with his piercing eyes. A little while later he set her down on the rocks on top of the sea lion exhibit. But, unlike the first time, there was plenty of room. She was the only one there.

Wendy waited for the others to arrive and thought about her birthday and the upcoming year. She smiled. With her new friends at LATCH and her new friends at school, Wendy had never been more hopeful about the future.

Still, no on else had arrived. The eagle was waiting,

just staring at her. Then Wendy noticed that he had something in his giant curved beak. Whatever it was glowed on this starlit night; it was yellowish and eerie.

Cautiously, Wendy touched the pale object. The minute she did, the eagle opened his beak, releasing the pale paper into her hand. It appeared to be a round map of the moon with writing hidden in the shadows.

The new moon's up, the time is here
To finish up your New Moon year.
The Quest is set, just made for you.
The seals will help you find your clue.

Use what you've learned night after night,
And face your foe, you'll be all right.
You know just how to be your best
So dig down deep, enjoy your Quest!

A spurt of adrenaline rushed through Wendy. "This is my Galileo Quest, isn't it?" she asked the bird excitedly. Without moving a chiseled feather on his arrogant head, his beady eyes shifted toward her ever so slightly. Then, he lifted his great stone wings and flew off.

"I don't know how April does it," Wendy muttered to herself. "Animals just don't seem to want to talk to me."

Well this is it, she thought. She had been so sure that the Galileo Quest would happen on the night of a full moon. But, as so often happened, her careful analysis had led her to the wrong conclusion. Since she was in the New Moon phase, her final challenge was obviously going to be on the night of a new moon.

She looked around wondering how to proceed.

That's when she became aware that she was surrounded by swirling water. To get out of here, she was going to have to go through the water.

To avoid looking at the water, she studied her moon clue. It looked like a hand-drawn map of the craters and seas of the moon. No doubt it was a copy of one of Galileo's maps. Nice touch.

Her peripheral vision caught sight of the water again. Her muscles tightened. She knew enough to realize that she couldn't possibly swim unless she was relaxed. She willed herself to breathe. She gave herself a pep talk. She could do it.

But first, she had to find her clue. The note said the seals would help her. All right. Carefully, she climbed closer to the water.

"Hey, Scooter, Seaweed, April," she called out.

Much more friendly than the eagle, the sea lions came leaping out of the water almost immediately. They barked as they rose in an apparent greeting of some sort. Wendy just shook her head. April understood what they were saying, but Wendy didn't have a clue.

Then it occurred to Wendy that the sea lions might be smarter than her. Maybe they could understand her, even if she couldn't understand them. "Can you help me find my clue?" she called out.

Seemingly eager to help, the sea lions jumped out of the water and waddled up to her. They were exactly like her three boys, all talking at the same time. If only April were here, she thought.

After several minutes of high-pitched barking, the sea lions seemed to realize that they were getting nowhere with Wendy. They stopped and dove back into the water.

Wendy was stumped. She could see nothing that

resembled a clue. She sat on the rocks, feeling miserable. And then, something came over her. This was ridiculous. She knew what to do, but she didn't want to. Her clue said it as plain as day.

She walked down to the water again. "Seaweed?" she called out softly. One sea lion jumped out of the water right away. "Take me with you to find my clue."

As if she understood perfectly, Seaweed stretched out one flipper. Bravely, Wendy took hold of it. Before she could think about what she was doing, Seaweed had pulled Wendy into the water.

At first, Wendy was so scared that she couldn't open her eyes. But Seaweed seemed to understand that she had to be gentle. Finally, Wendy managed to open her eyes. Since there was no visible moon, very little light made it through the depth of the water. It was dark and cold and unsettling.

Suddenly, Wendy spotted a speck of light on the very bottom of the pool. It was round and iridescent—she had found it!

Wendy tugged on Seaweed's flipper, trying to communicate that she wanted to dive down deeper. But the opposite happened. Seaweed swam to the surface and climbed out onto the rock.

"Please take me down to the clue," Wendy said.

The sea lion barked adamantly and pointed her flipper at Wendy.

Wendy tried to take her flipper. But in a flash, Seaweed wriggled out of Wendy's grasp and dove into the pool.

Once again, Wendy was afraid that she understood all too well what she was supposed to do. The clue had said that she should *face her foe,* her enemy, her fear. She was supposed to get the clue at the bottom of the pool by herself.

She stared at the note. *Use what you've learned, night after night.* She tried to focus, to believe that she could do it. Finally she walked down to the water and slipped in. She held her breath and dove down as far as she could. Her fingers were nowhere near the clue. She came to the surface sputtering.

This feeble attempt was never going to work. Really angry with herself for being so afraid of the water, Wendy made up her mind, clamped her arms next to her body and concentrated with all her might on becoming a sea lion.

Almost immediately, she arched deep down into the water and became a sleek swimming machine. Too fast, she came upon the clue and missed it. The next time around, she hovered over the spot just long enough to grab it.

In her joy, she zoomed out of the water and shot three feet into the air. Luckily, she splashed back into the water and not onto the brutal rocks.

Panting, triumphant, Wendy jumped out of the water holding the clue. She couldn't believe it. She had done it! All by herself. With no April. Diana was right. This was a wonderful game.

Almost as an afterthought, she looked at the clue.

You've done it, Wens, defeated fear.
You've found your clue, let out a cheer!
We thought you would, you have the heart,
Especially with an easy start.

But, now move on, the night is new.
Go to a place where it was blue . . .
Where Cleo walked and cobras met
There is a moat, so don't get wet.

A sea of wealth meets there tonight.
The diamonds sparkle very bright.
Eclipse has taught you how to score.
So, use your stuff, get in the door.

Wendy shivered as she stared at her next clue. Of course, she knew where she had to go next. The place where it had been *blue* with *Cleo* and *cobras*. The Blue Moon Ball at the Temple of Dendur at the Metropolitan Museum.

Her first task was to get across the water to the steps. She jumped in and swam over to the steps. "Goodbye April, Scooter and Seaweed. You were great. Thank you for all your help."

On cue, the three sea lions flipped out of the water at exactly the same time and barked.

Chapter Thirty-nine

Wendy walked as quickly as she could across the park to the Metropolitan Museum. She came to the front steps and stopped. Huge, shiny black limos lined the entire block. Oh dear, she thought, there must be some kind of incredible party here tonight.

A guard was waiting by the center door. But Wendy had another idea. In the shadows, Wendy climbed up the side. She flashed her moon key on the locked door and it opened with no resistance.

Soon she was on the balcony high over the Temple of Dendur. She looked down. *A sea of wealth* filled the gigantic room. She spotted the mayor, a senator and several well-known celebrities.

Her clue said *Where Cleo walked and cobras met.* Wendy knew instinctively that her next clue was hidden in the temple. She would have to pass hundreds of people in tuxedos and ball gowns. In her white slacks and blue top, she would stick out like a sore thumb. How in the world was she going to get there?

She had two major problems: her age and her

clothes. Thank goodness she was tall for a fourteen-year-old. But how could she look like she was dressed for a formal party?

She looked around frantically for some solution. The balcony had obviously been used for an earlier reception. Small tables covered in white lace tablecloths dotted the space. Wendy had an idea.

Her heart pounding, Wendy snuck downstairs and slipped into the ladies room. Somehow, in a stall, she managed to tie the tablecloth into a floor length lace skirt over her white slacks.

Now it was time for the really hard part of her transformation. She tried to fill herself with the assurance and confidence of the rich and powerful. She thought of Helena and Phillip. The tilt of their heads. The ease of their walks.

She remembered becoming Cleopatra and walking with the authority of a beautiful queen. She had done that. She had won the Blue Moon Prize. She could do it again.

Her chin up, her shoulders back, she pushed open the stall door . . . and froze. A white-haired lady was touching up her makeup.

The lady nodded regally at Wendy and smiled. "Hello," she said in a cultivated voice.

Wendy imitated the slight nod. "Hello." Wendy waited for the woman to cry out that she was an imposter. But the woman did nothing of the kind. She returned to the party.

Wendy had passed her first test. Knowing that she would fall apart if she hesitated, Wendy swept out of the ladies room and directly into the main room. Ever so slightly, she nodded at one of the guards at the door.

For one split second, she thought he was going to

question her. And then she remembered her secret weapon. A warm, assured smile illuminated her face. He smiled back. She was in.

So as not to call attention to herself, she slowly worked her way towards her goal. She crossed the small moat that guarded the temple. She almost gasped out loud when her arm brushed up against an Oscar winner. Wendy wished that Hannah was with her.

Knowing that she risked detection moving as a loner, Wendy prepared to duck into the temple. That was when she made eye contact with a man in a wheelchair talking to the mayor. She froze. He looked exactly like an older version of Phillip. He continued to stare at her.

She scurried into the darkness of the small temple. Easily, she spotted her next glowing moon clue tucked between a crack in the ancient stones. It was so dark, she had to move very near the opening to read it.

You've made the grade, your Cleo reigns
So now you're off for other gains.
A different kind, forget black tie,
To pinstripes blue, let's not be shy.

You've tried before to hit the ball
Alas, your bat just missed them all.
Tonight, you'll have to do your best
To hit a home run for this Quest.

I know you think it can't be done,
But don't give up, and have some fun.
Just think of Babe, or even Mickey
With them in mind, it won't be tricky.

Wendy was in a total panic. She was supposed to go to Yankee Stadium and hit a home run? That was ridiculous. How would she even get there? She'd have to take the subway. It would take a long time.

She thought about giving up right then and there and hiding in the temple until the party was over. That was when she spotted Phillip Huntington III through the opening. He had moved his wheelchair so that he could peer into the temple. He had a strange expression on his face.

She had to get out of there. How was she going to get past Phillip's father? In a panic, her mind filled with an image of Yankee Stadium. The sloping field, the blinding lights . . .

And then, she was standing at home plate, still in her lace tablecloth skirt. For a minute, Wendy was terribly disoriented. Then she realized what had happened. She had willed herself to Yankee Stadium. Just like the night of the Blue Moon Ball when she had willed herself to go home. This power had been inside of her all along.

It certainly would make the rest of her Galileo Quest go faster if she could transport herself to her next destination. She looked at the blue wall, so far away. On the other hand, she might never get to the next clue if she really had to hit a home run. In her heart of hearts, she knew she couldn't hit a ball out of Yankee Stadium.

A pitching machine was sitting on the mound. Deeply discouraged, she moved to the batter's box. There, waiting for her, was a bat. She looked around the enormous, empty stadium, all 50,000 seats. It was terrifying in its silence. She was completely alone.

A shiver went down her spine. How in the world

was she going to get out of this? She turned and tripped on her lace skirt. She ripped it off in disgust.

She couldn't do it. The Galileo Quest was too much for her. She had talked a big game, bragged that she wasn't worried. But she didn't have the guts to survive. With all her might, she willed herself to be back home in bed.

It didn't work. A niggling part of her brain wouldn't let her give up so easily.

Reluctantly, she picked up the bat and stepped into the batter's box. As soon as she held the bat on her shoulder, a ball came whizzing out of the machine. Wendy jumped back. The speed of the ball was so great that her hair fluttered in the breeze.

Truly petrified now, she scrambled out of the box. The pitching machine did nothing, almost as if it knew when to throw. Her heart still racing, but fascinated, she gingerly stepped back into the box. Nothing happened. She lifted the bat up. A second later, another fastball zipped past her.

Okay. She was beginning to get it. Breathing hard, she lifted the bat again. This time she swung and missed. After several more pitches, Wendy actually nicked a ball. It dribbled foul toward first base.

Already dripping with sweat, Wendy pulled her first clue out of her pocket. *Use what you've learned night after night.* Steeling herself, she glared at the machine. It made its wind-up noise and a ball came flying out. Wendy kept her eyes glued to the ball. She wasn't aware of swinging, but with a crack the ball went flying over second base. Now, with some frequency, she could make contact, but her hits were barely clearing the infield.

She flung her bat down and stomped over to the Yankee dugout. What a stupid and unrealistic challenge. Even though she was stronger from her double R and R, she didn't have the power to hit it that far.

She sat there with her arms crossed, pouting. She wondered how long it would be before someone from LATCH would release her from her Quest. Her mind wandered to her last clue. *But don't give up, just have some fun . . .*

She was doing exactly what her clue had told her not to do. She was having a rotten time, giving up.

Just think of Babe, or even Mickey. She thought about the photos of Babe Ruth and Mickey Mantle that she had seen. They were two of the greatest baseball players in history. In most of the pictures, they were smiling. They loved playing baseball.

A smile finally on her face, Wendy imagined that she was Babe Ruth. If she could be a sea lion, she could surely be the Babe. Eagerly, she jogged out of the dugout and grabbed her bat. Mightily, she swung it around her head. The crowd roared. They loved the Babe. She was a hero.

With arrogance, she swaggered into the box and crouched down. A ball came flying. Crack! The ball recoiled off of Wendy's bat. Higher, higher. Wendy was sure she had done it. And then, it died in the outfield.

Wendy stepped out, perplexed. It wasn't enough. She needed to visualize the pitcher, a pitcher she could destroy. This time, she didn't see the machine, she saw Phillip, smirking as he had when he had pitched to her. The night they had beaten him.

A grin spread across Wendy's face as she fully remembered that night. She didn't need to be the Babe; she could be Wendy. As the next pitch sailed toward her, Wendy willed it to slow down, until it was a nice fat beach ball. Her bat made contact with a commanding sound. Up, up, up, the ball went. Then gravity began to have its way. But this time, she focused on the ball with all her might, willing it to fly on with a life of its own. Just like she had moved the candelabra in Cloud Counting, the ball leveled off but continued right over the centerfield wall.

A deafening roar filled Wendy's ears. The scoreboard lit up. Sirens shrieked. Home run, home run! She had done it!

Wendy was wondering how to find her next clue when she noticed the scoreboard. A large yellow moon sparkled in thousands of lights. From inside the moon, words appeared and scrolled down.

We knew you could, despite your fears.
You've topped the wall to noisy cheers.
A mighty blast came off your bat,
Your clue is won, we tip our hat.

So brace yourself for your phase four.
We trust you're ready for some more.
You've used the skills you've learned at night.
Now hope will keep you in the fight.

Deep underground, the air is thick
With dust and grime that make sweat stick.
Just find the track that is the best
Then whisper soft, you'll hear the rest.

Realizing that she would only see this clue once as it rolled by, Wendy closed her eyes and tried to memorize it. She had learned by now that her clues were very helpful.

This time she had no idea where she was supposed

to go. So far, every clue had taken her to a place that she had been to in her first year at LATCH. This clue said, *Just find the track.* Where had she been with tracks? Her mind flashed to Eclipse. Could that be it?

Chapter Forty

It was dark and terribly hot. The air was filled with horrible smells and smoke. Wendy couldn't breath. What in the world was she supposed to do here?

Everywhere she looked she could see tracks, endless tracks meeting and crossing and continuing on forever. Wendy had no idea which way to go.

A powerful rumble started far in the distance, followed by a point of light. It got closer and closer. Wendy was paralyzed. At the last minute, the train veered inches away from her. Wendy was underneath Grand Central Station.

The light of the train had illuminated her underground prison. There were crackling electric cables and puddles of rusty water. A lethal combination. Now that the noise of the train had passed, Wendy could also hear scratching noises. She was terrified that they came from rats.

Wendy's skin crawled. She couldn't stifle a scream. It echoed down the decrepit tunnels. She had to get out of here.

That's when she noticed her moonstone ring. It was glowing, giving off a comforting light. For a moment, Wendy saw the twinkling eyes of the old woman who had given it to her. For the first time since arriving at Grand Central, Wendy felt a ray of hope.

Her heart leapt. This was a test of hope. That's what her clue had said. More calmly now, she inspected the labyrinth of tracks. She slipped her hand into her pocket and touched something hard. Her sister rock, from April. She had forgotten that she had put it there before her surprise birthday party.

Her fingers curled around it. She could feel the refreshing breeze on the French meadow. She could hear April's musical laughter. "Oh April," she whispered, "help me get out of here."

The rustlings and squeaks grew louder. She was sure now that rats were close by. Something above her seemed to move. She looked up. On the metal beam above her head, two green eyes appeared. Wendy thought she was hallucinating. She looked again. The eyes belonged to a cat who had obviously disturbed the rats. Could it be?

"Shadow, is that you?" she whispered.

The cat said nothing, but turned and curled her tail as if beckoning Wendy to follow her. Gracefully, the animal padded off.

Through tunnels and over beams, the cat led Wendy to a raised platform. Trembling, Wendy managed to pull herself onto it. Thankfully, she was finally out of the track bed and onto some relatively clean, dry cement. The rats seemed safely below.

She called out to the cat. "Thank you for leading me here."

But there were no green eyes. The cat had vanished. Wendy ran as fast as she could toward the light. She came out huffing and puffing into the lower level of Grand Central. Then she remembered the end of her clue. *Then whisper soft, you'll hear the rest.*

Slowly now, she walked up the ramp. She stood facing one of the corners.

"Hello," she managed in a breathless voice. "It's me, Wendy. What is my next clue?" She stood perfectly still, feeling like a fool. Then, in the softest whisper possible, she heard a reply:

You've stayed the course, you've made it
   through.
You didn't quit, your hope held true.
And now the last phase of the game . . .
We fear this part will seem quite tame.

Where turtles play and castles stand
A lovely pond is close at hand.
Just grab the oars, the boat is true
The Mystifier waits for you.

So back you go, to end your Quest
To cross the pond, to solve the test.
A year's gone by, so take a peek,
The mist contains the truth you seek.

Again, Wendy forced herself to remember the words. However, this one seemed a lot simpler. It even said itself that this part was *tame.* She had made it through the worst part.

She felt guilty, though. She was being rewarded for holding on to her hope, when that wasn't quite true. Without her moonstone ring, her sister rock, and, of course, the cat, she wasn't at all sure that she could have made it out. For the hundredth time, she wondered if Shadow was really April. But how could April have come to help her when she was undoubtedly on her own Galileo Quest? Anyhow, who knew if that cat was really Shadow.

The only thing that seemed clear was the answer to this clue. The pond by the castle where turtles play had to be Turtle Pond in Central Park.

With all her power, she willed herself to be out of the airless building and into the midsummer beauty of Central Park . . .

And, there she was. She took a long, deep breath of the sweet June night. The pond twinkled in the starlight. Belvedere Castle stood majestically on the rocks. The birds sang their nighttime fugues. A rowboat bobbed gently on the edge of the water.

Just grab the oars, the boat is true. Wendy's stomach flipped. This boat was waiting for her to cross the pond. For a weird moment, everything felt familiar. But that was impossible. She had always been terrified of the water. She had never been in a boat in her life.

She stared at the boat. Surely she could manage to row to the other side. It was certainly easier than getting to the bottom of the sea lion tank.

Bravely, she stepped into the rowboat and pushed off. The boat glided smoothly into the water. This was a piece of cake. Within a short time, Wendy had made it to the middle of the pond.

She stopped rowing. She felt so peaceful and joyful. She had to admit that she felt proud of herself. April had been right to worry. Every phase of the Galileo Quest had been designed to push her to her limits. But she had made it through.

Wendy was lost in her dreamlike thoughts when a large splash disrupted her tranquillity. What was that?

From the end of the pond, someone was swimming, speeding towards her like a torpedo.

Next thing she knew, the boat was nearly tipping over as Phillip yanked himself up on one side of it. Wendy screamed.

Phillip laughed, "Screaming will do you no good."

"What are you doing here? How did you know where I was? Aren't you on your Galileo Quest?" Wendy found that she was more furious than frightened.

Phillip held up his hand. "One question at a time . . . I took a little detour from my Quest. I thought we needed to talk. I had reason to suspect that you would be here."

"How?" Wendy fumed.

"Because this is exactly where my father encountered Serena on his Galileo Quest, where she destroyed his life. I knew you would be here. And, you see, I was right."

Wendy was afraid of Phillip's eyes. They glittered like glass. "Phillip, you've got to stop this. Petavius told me I have no connection to Serena. You've got to let go of this obsession."

"Petavius is protecting you, like he has from the start. I don't believe what he's said for a moment. I sensed from the beginning that you were trouble, the foster child who could do no wrong. But after your Cleo act and your telekinesis, I am convinced that your destiny is connected to mine, just as Serena's was to my father. I want you out of LATCH. I won't stop until you leave. I'll do whatever I have to."

Phillip's eyes bored into Wendy. At that moment, she knew for certain that he had gone after the boys and that he would happily do it again.

Her fury boiled up inside of her and she thrust an

oar at him with all her might. Never a violent person, she would have done anything to get rid of him.

But Phillip was too quick. He had anticipated this move. He grabbed the oar and pulled on it. She lost her balance and fell toward Phillip's side of the boat. The boat tilted alarmingly as they struggled.

Wendy stood up to try to regain control of the oar. That was her mistake. She lost her balance and toppled, crashing over the side.

For a second she was stunned. She was surrounded by black water. She gulped and flailed in panic. She kicked as hard as she could and rose to the surface. Her lungs felt like they were going to burst. Up and up, she went searching for the light, the surface. But it just got darker and darker. When she reached what should have been the surface, her head hit something hard. She was completely out of air. But, she felt as if Phillip had trapped her in a living, floating coffin.

Everything that had happened to Wendy in the last year flashed through her mind. For a split second, she felt like she was going to remember something, something important. She kicked and splashed like a baby. Her fear of water out of control, Wendy totally panicked, swallowed more water and began to black out.

Chapter Forty-one

Wendy felt herself slipping away, disappearing, just like she always had at school when no one would sit with her at lunch, when she got picked for teams as an afterthought because no one even realized she was there, when her foster families would forget her birthday. It was a feeling she was used to. It was a feeling she hated.

No! She was not that same invisible girl. She had come too far in her last year at LATCH. Suddenly, something from deep inside of her bubbled up. Almost like another breath of air. She stopped panicking.

Phillip couldn't have put her in a coffin. She was being ridiculous. Boldly, she reached up and felt what was blocking her from getting to the surface. It was the bottom of the boat. Of course. She kicked a few feet over and instantly her head broke into the delicious June night. Gratefully, she gulped the life-saving air.

Feeling restored but furious, she tried to get her

bearings. Where was Phillip? Every molecule of her being wanted to get him.

Suddenly she heard his laughter as she spotted the boat, already several yards away from her. "You're not afraid of the water, are you?" he taunted.

Powerfully, Phillip was rowing back to the shore where the boat had been waiting. Clearly he hoped to leave her to drown.

But Wendy was not going to do that. After all, just tonight she had swam with the sea lions and found her clue at the bottom of their pool. For a split second, Wendy's overriding impulse was to follow Phillip. But that really was stupid. It would be very hard for her to catch him. And even harder to climb into the boat to get to him.

Anyhow, she reasoned, she hadn't finished her Galileo Quest yet. She was supposed to *cross the pond, to solve the test.* And that's just what she was going to do. Phillip Huntington the Fourth was not going to stop her.

Using all her powers of concentration, she refused to think about how deep the water was, or what might be lurking in the darkness around her. It probably wasn't named Turtle Pond for nothing.

Hearing Persephone's voice in her head, she focused with all her might on the new moon that she knew was up in the sky even though she couldn't see it and the twinkling stars of hope that she could see.

She took a deep breath and began to swim.

Feeling more triumphant than she had ever felt, Wendy rose out of the water onto the bank on the other side of the pond. She had finished her Quest. The empty boat was bobbing on the other side of the water. Phillip was gone. It was almost as if he'd never been there.

The world was completely silent, except for the whispers of nature. Wendy looked around. That is when she spotted the glow coming from the terrace of Belvedere Castle.

She began to climb toward the light, knowing that was where she must end her Quest.

Petavius was standing next to the glow of the Moon Mystifier. His face was serious. "Congratulations on completing your Galileo Quest. You overcame all your fears."

"Thank you," Wendy responded. Did Petavius know what Phillip had tried?

"He came after you, didn't he?" Petavius interrupted her thoughts.

"He wanted me to drown. He won't stop. Until I'm gone," Wendy explained simply. For the first time, saying these words didn't scare her.

Petavius almost snarled. "Phillip was not part of your Quest. I'm sorry you had to face him like that. But I can deal with him. I was late getting here tonight. By the time I came, you had things under control."

Wendy smiled. "Yes, I did. I discovered something in me that I had no idea I possessed. I have LATCH to thank for that. LATCH has been the most fantastic thing that has ever happened to me. I have cherished every night that I've attended."

"Why are you talking like that, as if it is over?" Petavius snapped.

Wendy took a deep breath. It was very hard to say this to Petavius. "The Galileo Quest was amazing tonight. The tests were everything that I was most scared of. But I found every clue. And, in the final round, I even survived against Phillip. So I know that

I can hold my own against him. But I don't know what he'll do to my boys. I can't guard them every minute. I could never live with myself if anything happened to them."

Petavius ran his fingers through his hair, looking like an old man. Wendy wondered why he looked so sad.

"Please look at this," Petavius said suddenly, pointing to the Mystifier.

Wendy looked. She blinked. The mist swirled and formed into a smiling, attractive girl. This girl looked likeable, bright and fun.

"This is the Wendy as other people see you. Do you remember how you looked last summer? Do you realize how far you've come this year? The sky is the limit for you at LATCH," Petavius insisted.

Wendy had to agree that she was unrecognizable from a year ago. She thought about everything that had happened to her. Her new confidence, her new appearance, her new friends. She had come so far. It had to be enough.

"Isn't the main principle of LATCH that we all have the power in ourselves to become the best we can be?" Wendy asked calmly.

"Of course, I've said it many times," Petavius agreed impatiently.

"That was the most important lesson, and I understand it now. So you see, I can grow on my own, without LATCH."

Petavius turned red. "You have barely scratched the surface. You have no idea what you're giving up."

Wendy didn't doubt that Petavius was right. She knew there was so much more to learn. And, more than anything, she didn't want to miss all of the fun of LATCH. She would miss April and Pedro so much. Wendy looked at Petavius. "We both know that

Phillip has power, power from the dark side of the moon. I have to protect my boys. If you care for me at all, please let me go."

Petavius' face softened. "Of course I'll let you go, if that's what you really want. I can't make you attend LATCH. Each partipant has to be willing. But first let me ask you one question. Which do you think has the most power, the light or the dark side of the moon?"

Wendy searched her mind and her heart. "The thing is, the light side of the moon is the one that has charmed people for centuries. It has inspired people to paint, write poems, create myths, fall in love. . . . The dark side is really invisible. It is mysterious, unknown."

Petavius nodded. "And which side do you connect to?"

Wendy almost laughed at the absurdity of the question. "The moon shining in the darkness, of course. It's kept me going so many nights . . ." She fingered her necklace. "It seems to symbolize hope. That's what we've spent the whole year working on in Illumination. Hope, belief. Knowing that you can make things happen."

"So if Phillip identifies with the dark side and you with the light side, who is going to win?" Petavius asked softly.

Wendy stared at Petavius. Her mind raced over the last year when Phillip seemed to need to cheat to do well during revelations. How he begged her to help him light the Statue of Liberty's torch. How his Moon Mystifier had crackled and sparked. And just tonight, how he wasn't able to defeat her, despite her terror of the water. "I guess I might," she whispered.

Petavius just stared at her, challenging her with his eyes.

Wendy cleared her throat. "I will. I am stronger."

Petavius nodded with a smile. "Yes, you are . . . if you believe it."

"I do." Wendy's voice grew more confident. As she said those words, something in her knew that they were true.

"So you want to stay in LATCH," Petavius clarified.

"I want to stay," Wendy agreed definitely.

Petavius' face was illuminated by joy. Suddenly, he engulfed her in his strong arms and gave her a big hug.

Wendy was confused. Petavius had never acted like this before.

Petavius cleared his throat. "I've waited so long for this day. I've tried to protect you. But, I think now that you are strong enough, you are ready to hear. . . ."

Wendy had no idea what was going on. But, she knew that it was something important. "Ready to hear what?"

Petavius shook his head. "I know this is going to be a shock for you But the reason it is so important to me that you stay in LATCH is because . . . you are my granddaughter."

"What?" Wendy was too stunned to fully understand Petavius' words.

"I know this must seem impossible . . . ," Petavius murmured.

"Phillip kept telling me that you treated me differently. But I couldn't believe it," Wendy stammered.

Petavius looked chagrinned. "I tried to treat you the same as everyone else. But it was difficult. You are so much like your mother, Serena."

A chill went up Wendy's spine. How could this be true? "Serena is your daughter?"

Petavius shook his head at Wendy's natural confusion. "I thought of her as my daughter. But actually,

Serena was married to my son, Kane. They met at LATCH. They were your parents."

"*Were* my parents?" Wendy asked with a stone in her stomach.

"Yes. They're gone . . . ," Petavius said softly.

Wendy was bewildered. "I've never even heard of Kane."

"He was two years older than Serena at LATCH. As a matter of fact, he was her buddy. After LATCH, they fell in love and were married," Petavius explained.

Wendy couldn't breathe. Why was all this happening tonight? "Why did they abandon me?" she asked painfully.

"They loved you so much," Petavius tried to explain. "They felt it was the only way to keep you safe. It was the only way to protect you."

Wendy's heart thudded. Her parents had loved her. "They were protecting me from the Huntingtons, weren't they? Because of what happened between Serena and Phillip's father on his Galileo Quest?"

"There was bad blood between our families for years. It started between me and Phillip's grandfather. But after the incident at the Galileo Quest when Phillip's father got hurt, the Huntington family had a vendetta against Serena. They couldn't tolerate her being happy. When they learned that she was pregnant with you, they went after her again," Petavius explained painfully. He paused dramatically. "They tried to drown her . . . and you."

Suddenly everything was clicking into place. "Is that why I'm so terrified of water?" Wendy asked. "I never could understand why I was so afraid."

Petavius shook his head. "It was terrible. You and Serena almost didn't make it. That's when your parents made the unbearable decision to leave you."

"That's why Phillip has gone after me." Wendy was very shaken.

"Phillip has no idea who you are," Petavius interrupted firmly. "Your parents and I made sure that there has never been any connection."

"But he senses that I'm like Serena. What will he do when he finds out the truth?" Wendy worried.

"He won't. He can't. This will be our secret," Petavius promised.

Wendy gulped. This was the most important thing she had ever learned. She wanted to shout it from the rooftops. Yet she couldn't breathe a word.

"You can handle it. You are strong enough," Petavius assured her.

Wendy was beside herself. "I have finally found my grandfather, but I have to keep it a secret. I can never see you, be with my family. It seems so unfair."

For the first time Petavius laughed—a warm, loving laugh. "Oh, my dear, you underestimate me. Of course, we will find ways to be a family. I am not without my powers."

Wendy's face lit up. "Oh, I can't wait for that."

Petavius was concerned about Wendy. She looked so pale. "I know you must have a thousand questions, my dear. And, I will tell you all that I can. But, you've been through enough tonight. Get some rest. Savor your triumphs tonight."

Before Wendy could utter a syllable of protest, she felt Petavius drop a soft kiss on the top of her head. Then she heard the familiar whoosh.

Chapter Forty-two

The first rays of light were just creeping into her room when Wendy's eyes fluttered open. She squeezed her eyes tight, trying to clear her head. Her dreams . . . they had been so vivid, but so confusing. Suddenly, her heart started to pound as she began to remember the details. Her Galileo Quest, Phillip . . . her eyes suddenly snapped open as big as saucers. Petavius! Could it be true?

Knowing that she would not sleep another wink, Wendy opened her window and climbed out onto the roof. Pale peach and pink light streaked the sky. Wendy's eyes caught movement disappearing behind the chimney. What was that? It looked like a small, dark animal.

Curious, she was drawn to the spot. That's when a piece of paper fluttered, as if it were alive. As Wendy got closer, she saw it was a piece of wrapping paper next to a pile of gifts. Oh, her birthday party. She had almost forgotten. April . . . , Pedro . . . , LATCH. Her first birthday party. Could that have only been a few hours ago? It seemed like a hundred years ago. So much had happened. She felt dizzy.

What was real and what was not? How was she ever going to make sense of LATCH? Was she dreaming the whole thing? Had she imagined that Petavius was her grandfather because she so desperately wanted a family? Wendy's mind swirled like the rich colors in the sky. How would she ever know for sure?

"Hey." A soft voice made Wendy jump.

She whirled around. "What are you doing here?" Wendy gasped.

"I wanted to hear about your Galileo Quest. How did it go?" April asked, as if it were the most normal thing for her to be up on Wendy's roof.

"April? It's dawn! How did you get up here?" Wendy was so confused.

April grinned that same grin that Wendy remembered from their first night at the Central Park Zoo. Wendy had to laugh at how she had originally thought that April was a scared little thing. She was one of the most fearless people Wendy had ever met.

"Oh, don't worry about how," April said lightly. "It doesn't matter."

In a flash, Wendy thought of the shadowy movement that she had just seen behind the chimney. And then she remembered her Galileo Quest—the part at Grand Central. "Of course it matters," Wendy insisted. "You know perfectly well how my Galileo Quest went. You were there! At least for part of it. Why don't you just tell me the truth? Somehow, you can become a cat. I have no idea how that's possible, but that's how you got up here this morning. That's how you've delivered all those notes to me. That's how you helped me last night. I was so scared. But then I thought of you as I held onto my sister rock, and Shadow appeared and led me out of that nightmare." Wendy glared at April. "Who knows, maybe you can even turn into other animals."

"Sounds like fun," April teased, avoiding a serious response. "I'll have to try it sometime."

"You're not denying it, are you?" Wendy was not going to drop it. "I don't know why you can't tell me the truth. But I'll take your answer for a yes."

For a second their eyes met. "So how was the rest of your Quest?" April said.

"You know that too, don't you?" Suddenly, Wendy sensed that April had come at this unusual time for a reason.

"I've been worried about Phillip. I don't trust him," April admitted. "I kept tossing and turning last night. I think my bad dreams were about you and Phillip."

Wendy nodded. "Your instincts were right. Phillip tried to sabotage the last part of my Quest."

"Well, he obviously didn't succeed." April was pleased.

"No, he didn't," Wendy affirmed proudly. "But he won't give up."

"Well let him keep trying. He's got me to contend with, too," April claimed with bravado. "Not to mention Pedro and Petavius."

The mention of Petavius made Wendy freeze. How she wanted to tell April her amazing news. But she couldn't.

Of course, April noticed her reaction. "What is it?"

Wendy scrambled, "I'm just beginning to realize that being part of LATCH makes us a part of something much bigger. So many people have helped me this year." Wendy stared at her moonstone ring. "Even the old lady who gave me this ring."

"You never told me about that," April prompted, still curious about Petavius.

"It was pretty weird. During the holidays, I talked to this old lady on the subway. You know, how sometimes it's easier to confide in a complete stranger. She ended up giving me her ring. I was surprised when I learned it was a moonstone. And then tonight, it seemed to glow when I most needed it." Wendy talked fast, hoping to distract April from questioning her about Petavius.

"You're not the only one who's gotten help. My sister rock helped me, too, tonight," April said. "One of my challenges on my Quest involved lighting a candle at the Cloisters. You know me, I always tend to jump in without thinking. But this task involved being very quiet and concentrating. I thought of you. After what seemed like hours of struggling, my candle burst into flame."

Wendy felt her throat tighten. She'd never had a friend like April. They had shared so much at LATCH. "LATCH has been such an unbelievable experience for so many reasons. But, I think, becoming your friend has been the best part."

"Even if we don't tell each other everything," April teased, lightening the moment.

Wendy had to laugh. They knew each other well enough to know that they were both keeping something from the other.

"Just imagine the trouble we can get into during our next four phases!" April giggled with anticipation.

Wendy had a feeling she knew where the trouble was going to come from. She reached into her pocket, just as April was reaching into hers. Simultaneously, Wendy and April pulled out their sister rocks and held them in the palms of their hands. Side by side, the stones glowed with promise in the dawn's rosy light.

Wendy looked at April and smiled. "Phillip better watch out!"